"How long have you been standing there?"

Long enough, Virginia could have told Jordan, except that she knew he'd resent anyone having witnessed his brief lapse into humanity, or that moving exchange between him and his son. It had brought tears to her eyes, let alone his, but Jordan Caine wasn't the sort of man to view that as sympathetic consideration. More likely it would intensify his prickly hostility.

So she lied to him. "Not long at all. I came down the hall just as you were leaving Patrick's room."

Dear Reader,

My grandmother was a great believer in positive clichés and I was a great believer in my grandmother's wisdom. So it never occurred to me to doubt that even the blackest cloud was lined with gold or that, however bad things might seem today, they'd look better in the morning. I grew up believing that a glass half-empty is also a glass half-full.

Many years later I realized that of all the gifts my grandmother gave to me, the greatest was that she made me an optimist, a believer in tomorrow. Now a grandmother myself, I'm trying to pass on that gift to my little ones.

Sometimes, though, life deals out blows so cruel that a person can't—or won't—focus on the positive. Jordan Caine is in danger of becoming just such a man, so obsessed with avenging past injustices that he runs the risk of souring all the good things life has to offer. Virginia, my heroine, has known her share of trouble, too, but she's a "glass half-full" sort of woman. Just because the course of true love doesn't always run smoothly is no reason for her to turn away from it, and with a woman like that meddling in his life, even Jordan Caine finds he can dare to dream!

This book is for Ryan and Katie, my darling grandchildren who every day give to me far more than I can ever hope to return. May your lives be more full of sunshine than shadows, and your glasses always half-full.

Best wishes,

Catherine Spencer

SIMPLY
THE BEST
Catherine Spencer

Harlequin Books

TORONTO • NEW YORK • LONDON
AMSTERDAM • PARIS • SYDNEY • HAMBURG
STOCKHOLM • ATHENS • TOKYO • MILAN
MADRID • WARSAW • BUDAPEST • AUCKLAND

ISBN 0-373-03365-6

SIMPLY THE BEST

CHAPTER ONE

THE new owner of the mansion on the hill was not, Virginia decided, a very thoughtful man. In fact, he was downright inconsiderate. She'd been cooling her heels for the better part of half an hour, waiting for him to keep the appointment made at his convenience as long ago as last week. If it were any other client, she'd have left after ten minutes. Her time was too precious to waste. But this was a special house; it was—or used to be—her family's home.

It had been nearly a decade since she'd set foot inside its impressive, ivy-clad walls and, from the little she'd seen today, the years had not dealt kindly with the place. The once-gorgeous maple floors were dull, the French silk wall-coverings faded. She wasn't too surprised though; almost from the day Ted Connaught, the previous owner, had taken possession, neglect had begun to erode the splendour.

The interlocking-brick driveway inside the wrought-iron gates had become mired in fallen leaves, the manicured lawns choked with crabgrass and dandelions. Nothing remained of her mother's prize roses but an overgrown tangle of spindly shoots braided with thistles. The weather vane atop the gazebo had never been replaced after it blew down during a blizzard four winters ago and at least two of the shutters on the gatekeeper's cottage skewed crookedly from loose or broken hinges.

Virginia stood at the tall leaded windows in what used to be her father's library, and rubbed a tongue-dampened fingertip against a dusty pane. The stained glass borders glowed pink and mauve where the afternoon sun caught them.

'Shades of ruby and amethyst, my darling, and the shot fire of diamonds in the chandeliers...' She could almost hear the ghost of her mother's voice, cultured and refined like everything else from Virginia's privileged childhood. 'You might as well become familiar with your gems at an early age...'

Behind her, the door snapped rudely open. 'Sorry to keep you waiting, Miss Kent.'

He didn't sound remotely sorry. Virginia swung round, half inclined to tell him so, and found herself confronting another ghost. Not familiar like her mother, but a ghost nevertheless. The face, the eyes...where had she seen them before? And why did seeing them now cause her heart to skip a beat?

Recognition eluded her, slipping away before she could tie it to any specific memory.

He gave her hand a brief, impersonal shake and indicated a chair across from the sheet of plywood propped on two saw-horses that served as his desk. 'I'm Jordan Caine. Sit down, please. I've noted a few ideas somewhere here that I'd like to run through with you before we tour the house.'

'Mr Caine, I...um—have we——?'

He paused from sifting through the file in front of him and pinned her in a blue, unsmiling gaze. 'Is there a problem, Miss Kent?'

She hesitated, then shook her head. To ask him if they'd met before somewhere might well be interpreted as a clumsy attempt at flirtation, and she'd never felt less coquettish in her life. 'No,' she said. 'No problem.'

'Then let's get on.' He flung a glance at his watch. 'I don't have time to waste.'

'Nor I,' she told him, rather more sharply than was usual for her.

His faintly raised eyebrows told her he hadn't missed her rebuke. 'I want all traces of the old décor removed,' he stated dispassionately, running a well-shaped finger down the page before him. 'Everything will be done fresh. Get rid of the heavy velvet drapes at the windows and throw the mouldy old rugs left behind from previous owners in the trash can.'

'They're Chinese wool!' she protested. 'All they need is to be cleaned.'

'Miss Kent, I don't care if they're hand-embroidered silk. I want them out of here. If you find dumping them in the garbage too painful, feel free to donate them to your favourite charity.' He scanned the sheet of paper in his hand. 'The kitchen is to be gutted, also the bathrooms. Bring in a plumber and an electrician to check the condition of all pipes and wiring before you go ahead with cosmetic repairs.'

'Are you going to throw out the bathroom fixtures?' she enquired, in a voice that threatened to tremble.

He fixed her in his cool gaze once again. 'Do you seriously suppose otherwise?'

She swallowed. 'Are you aware that they're irreplaceable? That claw-footed cast-iron bathtubs fetch a small fortune in today's collectors' market, and that antique pedestal sinks and brass faucets are equally sought-after?'

'Penny-farthing bicycles are antique, too, Miss Kent, but I don't propose to ride around on one, nor, I venture to suggest, do you.'

Virginia didn't reply, mostly because she couldn't think of anything sufficiently insulting to fling in his face. Instead, to her chagrin, she felt like bursting into tears. You can't do this! she wanted to protest. You're erasing the best years of my childhood.

But the sad fact was, he could do whatever he pleased with the house, including razing it to the ground if it suited his fancy.

'You have the better part of two months to complete the make-over on the rest of the house,' he said, tapping a gold-capped pen on the calendar tacked to the wall next to him, 'but I want three bedrooms, at least one bathroom, the kitchen and the breakfast-room finished and ready for occupancy within three weeks. I've already hired a contractor to take care of the landscaping and pool area.'

'Three weeks?' Virginia practically squeaked the question at him. 'Impossible!'

'In that case, I'll find someone else to handle the work.'

'There *is* no one else—at least, not in Opal Lake.'

His smile would have been beautiful had it not been completely lacking in humour. 'The world doesn't start and end in Opal Lake, Miss Kent, and there is *always* someone else if the price is right.'

True enough, she thought. And God only knew what sort of botch someone else might make of redecorating the mansion. 'The rooms will be ready,' she promised rashly. 'Three weeks from today, you'll be able to move in.'

'Fine,' he said. 'The job is yours.'

She stared. 'Don't you want to know what it'll cost?'

He waved a bored hand. 'It doesn't signify. Do the job, Miss Kent, and do it well—oh, yes, and one more thing.' He regarded her with the sharp intelligence of a blue-eyed wolf on the prowl. A lofty, intimidating glance that briefly impaled her before dismissing her as being infinitely unworthy of entrapment. 'Make a point of using the side door in future—the tradesman's entrance, I believe it used to be called in the old days.'

She'd never crossed that threshold once in all the years she'd lived in the house. The way he ordered her to do so now was a calculated affront intended to insult her. She refused to give him the satisfaction of knowing he'd succeeded. 'As you wish, Mr Caine.'

'Good.' He stood up and indicated the door. 'Then let's proceed with the tour. I assume you brought along a notebook and pen?'

'Naturally. Also a camera and a sketch-pad. I'm very good at what I do.'

'So it would seem,' he replied. 'I checked out your references. You come very highly recommended.'

'Thank you.'

He raised his elegant black eyebrows again. 'For what? You've yet to do anything to earn *my* praise,' he informed her, and strode down the hall toward the breakfast-room and kitchen.

Virginia followed him and wished uncharitably that he'd slip and break his neck on the marble-tiled floor.

David was sitting on the porch, facing the lake, when she got home nearly four hours later. Lucas lay at his feet, aristocratic black nose resting on his paws.

'Well?' Without turning his head, David smiled. 'How was it? Were you swamped with *déjà vu* as you strolled the halls of the old homestead?'

Dropping into the chair next to him, Virginia expelled a long, heartfelt sigh and closed her eyes. 'It was... dreadful.'

David turned slightly, his head tilted to one side. 'Virginia? Have you been crying?'

'Only on the inside.' She touched his arm reassuringly and looked around. 'Where's Susan?'

'At the dentist's, having her six-month check-up. She mentioned it at breakfast this morning, remember?'

'I'd forgotten.' And small wonder! A lot had happened since breakfast.

'You sound disappointed,' David said lightly. 'What's the matter, don't I measure up as a substitute for your favourite confidante?'

'Don't be silly,' Virginia protested. 'No one could ever take your place with me, not even Susan.'

Nevertheless, there was a grain of truth in what he'd said. Susan was so sensible, so balanced in outlook, it was small wonder Virginia and David both had fallen into the habit of confiding in her. Who'd have expected, six months ago, that the young woman they'd hired to help run the kennels and take over some of the household duties would so quickly establish a special place in their hearts? She'd become part of their small family, the sister Virginia had never had as a child.

'Well, then?' Concern lent David's voice a sharper edge. 'What *has* got you sounding so down?'

'It's the new owner. David, he's...' again, Virginia hesitated, searching to do justice to the absolute horribleness of the man who was to be their neighbour as well as her client '...absolutely horrible,' she finished lamely, incapable of finding the words to convey the extent of her antipathy, or Jordan Caine's unspeakable arrogance. 'I can't imagine we're going to agree on a single point. Would you believe he wants to send Mother's Chinese rugs to the dump? Or that he's throwing out the plumbing fixtures?'

'Tell him you'll buy them from him,' David said calmly. 'If we can't find a place for them here, you can always sell them to a more discerning client later on.'

'I offered,' Virginia told him. 'And he looked at me pityingly and said, "My dear Miss Kent, take them with my blessing if they're that important to you, but don't insult me by expecting me to take money for them." I felt like a beggar at the door asking for alms.'

'You know, I had a feeling all this was going to be harder on you than you thought, so I got Susan to set everything out before she left for her appointment.' David slid his hand over the surface of the table beside him until his fingertips made contact with the tray that held glasses and decanter. 'Why don't you pour us some sherry, Sis, and tell me about this brash newcomer?'

'He's much younger than I expected—about thirty-six, I'd guess. Tall, very dark—and very handsome, I suppose. Curly black hair cut short, olive skin—the kind that never burns in the sun—and rather extraordinary blue eyes with shades of lavender in their depths. A bit like——'

'Michaelmas daisies.' David nodded. 'I remember.'

'But darker than that. Very intense, David, and searching, somehow.'

'Probing?'

'Yes, and guarded. No emotion there. The same with his smile.' Virginia closed her hands around the cool crystal neck of the decanter. 'Perfect—but completely without warmth.'

'A very reserved man, from the sound of it. Is he married?'

She poured two glasses of sherry and placed one in her brother's hand. 'Yes. At least, I assume so. One of the bedrooms is for his son who's five.' She clinked her glass lightly against David's. 'Poor little thing, with a father like that!'

'He might not be so bad, once you get to know him better.'

Virginia shuddered. 'I really don't *want* to get to know him better, thanks.'

Amusement brimmed in David's voice. 'You mean you aren't planning to have him over for tea?'

'Not in the foreseeable future, no. And I doubt he'd come, even if I were. He's the most dreadful snob, David. He told me to use the tradesman's entrance the next time I go over there.'

David laughed aloud at that. 'Did he appreciate the irony?'

'I didn't bother to enlighten him. As far as he's concerned, I'm just the home fashion consultant hired to make the place over. And heaven knows, it needs it!'

'Well, you more or less expected it would, didn't you? I mean, it's no secret that the Connaughts didn't look after the property. They didn't even look after the mine, and if this new man manages to revive *that* and put the men in this town back to work, we can forgive him his lack of social graces.'

'Oh, I wouldn't say he's exactly lacking in those,' Virginia said, recalling the cool courtesy with which Jordan Caine had opened doors for her and extended a helping hand over the stack of lumber where the carpenters had been repairing the floor in the ballroom—and trying not to recall the electric touch of his strong, capable fingers closing over hers. 'He's just...a snob. But the oddest thing of all is, I felt, when I first saw him, as if I'd met him before, yet I can't place him.'

'Does his name strike a chord?'

'No.' Virginia frowned. 'Not at all. I wish you could see him, David. You might remember.'

'Maybe I'll go over and introduce myself when he moves in. His voice might bring something back.'

'Thank goodness you'll have Lucas with you. You might need him to defend you against the big bad wolf.'

Hearing his name, the four-year-old German shepherd pricked up his ears and swivelled his eyes in Virginia's direction. David reached down and stroked his head. 'Maybe you should take him yourself, the next time you go over. It would be interesting to see if Lucas dislikes Mr Caine as thoroughly as you do.'

It occurred to Virginia then that what she felt for Jordan Caine was rather more complex than mere dislike. She found him insufferable of course—who wouldn't?—but there was a thread of something else involved, too; a vague trepidation laced with peculiar fascination. Something like the delicious fear she experienced watching a thriller on the television, one in which the villain never quite emerged from the shadows, yet one knew that he was never far from the heroine.

But if her feelings toward Jordan Caine were strangely ambivalent, there was little doubt about his for her. He didn't like her. She knew that, but she didn't know why. Nor did she know how he could have arrived at such a conclusion based on their brief acquaintance. Unless she'd been right and they had met before today. But if so, when? And where? And what had transpired between them that he remembered her with such ill will?

*   *   *

Virginia Mary Alexandra Kent hadn't recognized him, but even after thirteen years he could have picked her out in a crowd. The same flaxen silk hair, the same wide and wondering gray eyes framed in sooty lashes, the same delicate spun-sugar features. Still a princess, the only difference being that now she was a woman and then she'd been a girl—that, and her altered circumstances, of course.

He blinked at the column of figures on the page in front of him, as though doing so would erase the indelible picture of her stamped in his mind. He'd thought of her altogether too often over the last three days. She was becoming a nuisance—or else he was losing his grip.

Determined to ignore her intrusion, he paced to the window, lifted the corner of the Irish lace curtain, and scowled at the street below. Neat and narrow, just like the room behind him. A row of shops, each selling its ethnic specialties, with small residential apartments above, but the spit and polish of the old days were gone. Now, awnings hung tattered around their edges, painted trim flaked in places, and the occasional window was boarded over. A sign, not just of the times, but of too long a time for people who'd never been afraid to put in a hard day's work to earn an honest dollar.

All that was about to change, though. He'd see to it personally. He wasn't completely without redeeming qualities and hadn't come back solely for the satisfaction of teaching the Kents a lesson in humility. Within the year, he'd bring prosperity back to this neighborhood or die in the attempt.

A figure turned the corner, shoulders bowed by the weight of the shopping bags hanging from each hand. Cursing softly, Jordan crossed the room and hurried down the apartment stairs to open the side door.

'For God's sake, Momma, why didn't you get Lorenzo's to deliver all this?'

'To save money, Joey, why else?' His mother relinquished the load of groceries and fixed him in a reproving stare.

Jordan swallowed his irritation. 'You don't have to count the pennies any more, Momma. I told you, life's going to be easy from now on.'

'Easy?' She panted up the stairs ahead of him, a little thicker through the waist and hips than she had been when she was younger. 'What is easy, my Joey? Easy is not getting a phone call late at night to tell you that your baby granddaughter and her mother are dead in a car. Easy is not having to see the pain in your grown boy's face when he looks at a little white coffin and blames himself. Easy is when a man's ambition to succeed doesn't drive him away from his son.'

Was this the time to give her the facts? Caught in the same old dilemma, Jordan debated justifying his actions regarding his son by admitting that his marriage had fallen apart and that Penelope had been leaving him the day she and their daughter had died. That his wife, born to wealth and unable to adjust to a less extravagant lifestyle, had run up huge debts it had taken him nearly two years to pay off. And that the reason he was an acclaimed expert now was that he'd taken on the most difficult mining projects anywhere in the world, and worked seven days a week under appalling conditions, to make enough money to restore his credit rating *and* to ensure that Patrick would never find himself trapped in the endless grind of poverty that, despite his parents' best efforts, had blighted Jordan's early life.

No, he simply couldn't do it. It would sound too much like a condemnation of his own father, who had lacked both the education and the physical stamina from which Jordan had profited. Better Maria should harbour her misconceptions and thereby preserve her cherished illusions.

It was, however, time to establish the new order of things. Jordan was not about to let his mother think, just because they'd be living under the same roof again, that they would revert to their old parent-child relationship. The roles had been reversed now; he was the care-giver and the one who set the rules, not she.

'Let me remind you that, if it weren't for my ambition to be the best in my field, you might well be spending the rest of your life in this miserable apartment,' he pointed out, shifting the bags to one hand and reaching over her shoulder to hold open the door. 'As for Patrick, I could hardly have taken a three-year-old with me when I was working on-site all over the globe. I had no choice but to leave him with his grandparents.'

'I'm his grandparent, too,' Maria reproached him. 'You could have left him with me, then he would have grown up knowing that his father is a good man who loves him.'

'No, I couldn't have left him with you.' Jordan tried with poor success to subdue his impatience. 'He'd have worn you out in a week. At least the Winslows could afford to hire someone to help take care of him, which is more than I could do at the time. And for God's sake, Momma, stop looking at me as if I left him in a basket on the steps of some cold, Dickensian orphanage! I did the best I could, given the circumstances, and it was only for eighteen months. Now I'm in a position to make things up to him, so for all our sakes just let it rest.'

She removed her scarf and unbuttoned her coat, indisposed, it seemed, to allow him to deflect her attention. 'Put the past to rest?' She shook her head, and looked up at him from large, liquid eyes. Even at sixty-three, she retained traces of the beauty that had captured his father's heart. 'I don't think so, Joey. Not as long as you feed the anger.'

'I'm not angry,' he snapped, 'so let's talk about something else.'

She shrugged and turned to unpack the items in her shopping bag. 'Whatever you say, my son.'

'And never mind fussing with all that. I'm taking you out for dinner. We'll drive over to the house and you can see where you'll be living in another few weeks, then we'll go somewhere nice to eat.'

'My cannelloni isn't good enough, now that you're rich and powerful, is that it?'

Jordan came up close behind her and put his hands on her shoulders. He could smell her home-made shampoo, the one she'd always used. Balsam and lemon mixed with green soft soap. It took him back to his boyhood and reminded him why he had worked so hard to get where he was today. 'I want to make up for the hard times, Momma. Let me do that, please.'

'You came home,' she said. 'That makes up for a lot. If you can learn to be happy, it will make up for the rest.'

'No.' He gave her a little shake. 'You deserve better than this. I want you to enjoy life. I want other people to do things for you, for a change. Beginning with me. So what do you say, Momma? Will you wear your new black dress and be my date tonight?'

'Do I have a choice?'

He grinned. 'No. But you brought me up to be polite, so I thought I'd better ask.'

She planted her fists on her hips. 'You should smile like that every day, then I would soon have a daughter to love and we would have good reason to go out and celebrate.'

'You've got me, and once the house is habitable you'll get your wish and have Patrick, too. That's going to have to be enough.' He slapped her playfully on the behind. 'Go put on your fancy duds, woman. You're keeping me waiting.'

'Keeping the powerful Mr Jordan Caine waiting?' She hissed in a breath. 'I'm shaking in my boots!'

'The wiring's sound, Virginia, but I've got a feeling that's the only good news you'll be hearing today. The last I saw of Ed, he was coming down from the bathrooms and heading for the basement, and if the look on his face was anything to go by I'd say the new boss is in for a major overhaul of the plumbing.'

Virginia rolled her eyes and Barclay Finnings laughed. 'Just be glad you're not footing the bill on this one, Miss Interior Decorator, or whatever fancy name people like you go by these days. All you have to do is order the goods and let the boss cough up the dollars.' Barclay shrugged his shoulders and laughed again. 'No big deal, if the rumours about him are true. The jungle telegraph hasn't stopped beating since he blew into town.'

Virginia fought a swift and losing battle with professional rectitude. Making a final notation of floor measurements in her book, she perched on the recessed window-sill and encouraged the electrician to satisfy a curiosity which had grown steadily over the last three days. 'Exactly what *are* they saying about him, Barclay?'

'Well, you do know who he is, don't you?'

'Of course. The new owner of the mine.'

'No, no, Virginia. Before all that, I mean.'

'Before all what?'

'The letters behind his name, and the designer suits, not to mention the big fancy car he drives.'

A muted swish on the driveway below caught Virginia's ear. Glancing over her shoulders, she stiffened and slid off the sill. 'As in a dark emerald Lincoln mark VIII coupé sort of fancy car?'

'Yeah. Why?'

'He just pulled up outside. Better look busy, Barclay, if you don't want your ear chewed off.'

Grabbing her notes, measuring tape and sketch-pad, Virginia scooted down the hall to the second-largest bedroom. Overlooking the back gardens and pool, it had its own bathroom and also a pretty little sitting-room with leaded glass doors leading to a small balcony. Situated directly across the hall from the master suite, it had been her mother's room during the last ten years of her life.

Unhappy years, Virginia thought, remembering the shadowed tears in her mother's eyes, and her father's long, unexplained absences which made sense only when he brought his mistress to the house within weeks of burying his wife.

A wicker *chaise-longue* stood in one corner, dusty and forgotten against the delicate striped wallpaper. Underfoot, the dense pile of a white Chinese rug showed the careless imprint of workmen's boots. Here were two items, Virginia decided, that she wasn't too proud to salvage. For now, they could be stored in the unused third garage with other cast-offs from the house. Later, with Jordan Caine's permission, she'd haul both away and make them again part of her and David's life.

'A suite of rooms just for me? Too extravagant, Joey! Our whole apartment, kitchen and all, would fit into less space.'

The voice filtered through Virginia's preoccupation. Opening her pad at random, she busied herself sketching the sitting-room fireplace and the decorative cornice edging its mantel. Two sets of footsteps drew closer, and she knew the instant that Jordan Caine's eyes made contact with her back. Her spine tingled as though a fine, live electric wire threaded from one vertebra to the next.

'Ah, Miss Kent.' His voice had a less subtle effect, abrading her nerve endings unpleasantly. 'I was wondering where you were hiding.'

She looked up from her drawing and spared him a cursory glance. 'I'm not hiding, Mr Caine, merely too busy to run down to greet you.'

'Well, it wouldn't have been your place to do that, now would it?' he replied silkily. 'You're not the lady of the house, after all. My mother, however, is. Allow me to introduce you. Momma, this is Miss Kent. I hired her to turn this drab old mausoleum into a home for us.'

Incredibly wise and lovely eyes, as warmly brown as his were glacially cool, inspected Virginia. 'But I know you!' Mrs Caine exclaimed, her plump face wreathed in smiles. 'You're little Virginia.' She clapped a hand to her mouth. 'Or am I supposed to call you Miss Kent now that you're all grown up?'

Virginia couldn't help smiling back. 'Please don't,' she said. 'I'd much rather be called Virginia.'

'And I'm Maria—but you probably don't remember that. I sewed your first party dress, and all your mama's ballgowns.' She inspected Virginia again. 'You're like her, but I suppose you already know that. Everyone must tell you the same thing. So fair, so pretty. Peaches and cream, Joey, wouldn't you say?'

He looked so rigidly frozen with horror that Virginia almost collapsed in giggles. 'Momma!' he protested.

Maria Caine sighed with comical resignation. 'So I forget I'm supposed to behave like royalty. What do you expect? I'm an old woman, too set in my ways to change them now.' She wandered from sitting room to bedroom and back again. 'So, Virginia, this is what a suite looks like, eh? What am I supposed to do with so much space, play bingo with my friends? I'm a simple woman, you understand?'

'Don't worry. I'll make sure you feel comfortable here, Mrs Caine.'

Maria Caine tipped her head to one side and inspected the bare walls. 'Tell me what you think would look best.'

'It's what you think that counts, Momma. Miss Kent's job is to please you, not herself.' Jordan Caine grasped his mother's elbow and steered her back the way they'd come. 'We'll talk about it over dinner.'

'Bring her with us, Joey, then we can all talk together. Virginia——?'

Mrs Caine half-turned, her smile undimmed. Over her head, her son sent his employee a killing glare. 'I'm afraid I have a prior engagement, Mrs Caine,' Virginia said, 'but I'll be happy to meet with you some other time.'

'For sure. We'll make a date. And remember, my name is Maria.'

Jordan Caine's scowl lanced her so sharply, Virginia wouldn't have been surprised to see blood spurt forth. 'Ah...yes,' she murmured diplomatically. 'I won't forget.'

Just briefly, as their footsteps faded, Virginia remained rooted to the spot, trapped again in elusive memories. *Joey*...Joey... The name rang a distant summer bell, full of sunlight and laughter and excited childish voices. Balloons, a circus clown, birthday candles...

The front door slammed shut, startling her.

Muttering furiously, Virginia stuffed her supplies into her briefcase. Jordan Caine could have no possible association with such pleasant recollections. He was too caustic, too irascible; so much so that his precious project could go on hold until tomorrow. Just being in the same room with him had been enough to sour today's creative talents beyond redemption.

Whirling around, she started for the door, intending to make a speedy exit. And was brought up short by the sight of Jordan Caine's tall, broad-shouldered frame blocking her passage.

'And just where do you think you're going?' the object of her displeasure enquired, in that aggravating, autocratic manner of his.

CHAPTER TWO

HE MARCHED into the room and came to a halt close to where she stood poised for flight, making escape impossible unless she slithered around him. She was not prepared to do that.

'I'm finished for the day,' she said, with a bravado that was far from genuine, 'so I'd appreciate it if you'd let me by.'

'Not on your life,' Jordan Caine said. 'Not until we arrive at a precise understanding of the exchange that occurred in here a little while ago.'

'This really isn't necessary,' Virginia assured him. 'I understood it perfectly. You don't want me to forget my place. You want me to show you the proper respect.'

'Not to me. To my mother.' His tone was quiet, intense. 'You will not take advantage of her amiable nature. You——'

Virginia expelled an exaggerated breath. 'There's no need to bully me on your mother's behalf, Mr Caine. I have the utmost respect for her and will do my very best to accommodate her wishes as far as her rooms are concerned.'

'You'll do more than that,' he declared, still in the same deadly voice. 'You'll...direct her.'

'*Direct* her?'

He flushed slightly beneath his natural tan. 'Perhaps that isn't exactly the right word. Let's just say her options in the past have been limited. She is not accustomed to luxury, and I want you to act as her mentor. By all means consult with her, invite her suggestions—but, at the same time, broaden her horizons. Steer her, if need be, to choices that will result in her quarters being a fitting reflection of her status as the matriarch of this house.'

'Quarters?' Virginia couldn't help taunting him. 'I tend to associate that word with servants rather than mothers.'

He covered the last three or four feet that separated them with alarming speed. 'You forget yourself, Miss Kent. *You* are the hired hand here, not my mother, difficult though that may be for you to accept.'

'It's not difficult at all,' Virginia informed him. 'I'm rather proud of my expertise, and it doesn't bother me one iota to sell you the benefit of my professional training and natural good taste.'

His hand snapped up before she could guess his intent, and manacled her wrist. 'It's exactly that sort of remark that necessitated this discussion in the first place, Miss Kent. Your opinion of yourself and your talents is of no consequence. Your suggestions pertaining to this house, on the other hand, might possibly be considered relevant, particularly as they apply to my mother's suite of rooms. There will be nothing gauche about their décor.'

'Why can't she have exactly what she wants in here, without my influencing her choice?'

'Because I think she'll benefit from your wider experience and more exotic tastes,' he said smoothly. 'Why else would I have bothered to hire you?'

Virginia didn't know what possessed her. Some demon of mischief, possibly—or a self-destructive bent she hadn't been aware of previously. Regardless, the words fell out of her mouth before she could contain them. 'Because she's not as sophisticated as you'd like her to be and you're secretly ashamed of her, perhaps?'

She knew at once that she'd gone too far. If the sudden tightening of his rather delectable mouth hadn't been indication enough, the stormy blue of his gaze was. He yanked her closer; so close that she could almost count the profusion of dense black lashes rimming his eyes. 'I have no reason to be ashamed of either of my parents,

Virginia Mary Alexandra. Can you say the same about yours?'

Her mouth fell open in shock. 'What have *my* parents to do with this?'

Without exerting any sort of painful pressure on her wrist, he brought her up hard against him. His chest was about as yielding beneath the impact as a stone wall. She could smell his cologne, an expensive, subtle blend of spice and leather; could feel the staccato blast of his breath, mint-flavoured against her mouth. And for one wild, improbable moment she thought he was going to answer by kissing her.

But he didn't. Instead he let her go. 'Nothing,' he said, and turned away.

'Wait a minute!' She grabbed at his sleeve to detain him. 'You're not getting off that easily.'

He looked down at her fingers clutching the slubbed silk and wool of his jacket as though he found her touch unspeakably offensive. 'I beg your pardon?'

'What do you know about my parents? And how do you know my full name?'

At first, he seemed disinclined to reply. He raised his eyes and examined her face, feature by feature, his expression betraying nothing of what he was thinking. Finally, a sort of abbreviated sigh escaped him. 'You don't remember me, do you?' he asked.

'No—yes! Well, sort of. That is, when I first saw you the other day, there was something familiar about you. Then, this afternoon when I met your mother, I realized that you're not really new to Opal Lake, that this town was your home at one time. But I still can't quite place you.'

'That's because I never *had* any kind of place in your life, Miss Kent. None worth remembering, anyhow. At least, not until now. And believe me, you won't find me quite as forgettable this time around.'

Virginia failed to understand how she'd managed to do so the first time. So impossible a man was not easily dismissed from memory. She lifted her hands helplessly. 'You sound as though you want to punish me. Why? What did I do to make you dislike me so much?'

'Some time when I have nothing better to do, I'll enlighten you.'

'Why not now?'

'Because my mother is downstairs in my car and I'd rather keep you waiting than her. And because I'm paying you to work, not gossip.'

'I already told you, I'm finished here for today.'

'Really? How do you justify keeping such short hours when you're under so tight a deadline?'

'Don't worry, Mr Caine,' Virginia replied sharply. 'Your rooms will be ready for you on time. In three weeks, you'll be moving in.'

He didn't miss a beat. 'Wrong, Miss Kent. I'll be moving in in two weeks and four days.'

That demon of perversity rose up within her again. 'I'll make sure the red carpet's rolled out, Joey.'

His eyes flared dangerously, then, to her astonishment, his mouth curled up in the nearest thing to genuine amusement she'd yet seen in him. 'You're pushing your luck, Virginia,' he warned softly.

'And I suppose I was,' she told David and Susan over dinner that night, 'but strangely enough, I didn't feel the least bit threatened, even though he can be quite a terrifying presence when he chooses.'

'If he threatens you, overtly or otherwise, he's going to find *me* quite a terrifying presence.' David hefted his knife in one hand before setting it carefully on the side of his plate. 'And if his attitude toward you is typical of his manner toward employees, I can't see him making much of a success of the mine. He's going to need the co-operation of every man on the payroll, and the miners are already angry enough at past treatment. They won't put up with his sort of arrogance for a minute.'

'But he's not responsible for their having been out of work for the last year, David. As you pointed out the other day, they'll put up with almost anything as long as they can count on him to pay a regular wage at the end of every week.'

'Time will tell,' Susan remarked, barely able to quell the laughter in her voice. 'But what I want to know is, when did you start defending His Horribleness, Virginia? Have you changed your mind about him? Decided, maybe, that he's not so bad after all?'

'Hardly! He's rude, opinionated, arrogant, domineering——'

'The lady,' David observed, bursting out laughing also, 'doth protest an awful lot. Are you sure you're not secretly attracted to him, Sis?'

'There's nothing to be attracted to.' At least, not if a woman discounted lean muscular elegance and a simmering sexuality that it was impossible to ignore. Virginia drew in a shocked breath. 'No! Absolutely not. Anyway, he's married.'

'Just as well,' David said, sobering.

Susan began clearing the table. 'When are his wife and child arriving, Virginia?'

Virginia shrugged. 'He hasn't said. I assume he wants the house to be half-habitable before he sends for them.'

Actually, she was consumed with curiosity about the woman who was married to Jordan Caine. She wasn't able to satisfy it, however, until five days before her deadline fell due, when he showed up unexpectedly to check on the work in progress.

It was a Thursday, and one of those hot and hazy days not uncommon to mid-May in the interior valleys of British Columbia. The air outside was heady with the scent of lilacs in full bloom, and already the espaliered peach tree on the south side of the house was in bud. Birdsong trilled from every nook and cranny.

Inside the house, total chaos reigned. The kitchen cabinets, scheduled to be installed the following morning,

were stacked in the front hall cheek by jowl with crates
holding the new appliances and the bathroom fixtures
which the plumber was in the process of moving to their
permanent location. Permeating the entire atmosphere
was the odour of paint and polish, a fitting ac-
companiment to the profanities uttered by the various
other tradesmen left to crawl over and around the ob-
stacles barring their way as they raced against the clock
to put the final touches to Phase One of the make-over.

Not surprisingly, Virginia wasn't immediately aware
of Jordan's arrival. She was down on her hands and
knees placating Art Foley, who was repairing the maple
floor in the kitchen and cursing rather colourfully as he
did so. 'Don't know why you couldn't have settled on
sheet vinyl in here, Virginia,' he complained around a
mouthful of finishing nails. 'It'd be a damn sight cheaper
and a lot less bother.'

'Expense isn't a consideration,' Virginia said, 'and it'd
be a crime to cover up such beautiful wood.'

'You think I don't already know that, girl? But this
floor's been abused something fierce. Look at this mess
here—all warped where someone's flooded it with water.'

'I gather you've hit a snag,' a lone voice of calm observed, and Virginia looked up to find Jordan Caine
peering over her shoulder.

'Bloody right,' Art replied, unfazed by the fact that
he was addressing the most influential man in Opal Lake
with something less than awesome respect. 'Any damn
fool can see that.'

'I think the old dishwasher must have leaked,' Virginia
hastened to explain, scrambling to her feet and dusting
off her hands. 'The floorboards are rather badly
damaged and it's taking a bit longer than we'd expected
to make repairs.'

'I see.' Jordan took stock of the stripped room, noting
the taped electrical connections sticking out of the wall
and the plumbing pipes poking up through the floor. 'Is

that your diplomatic way of telling me you're running behind schedule?'

Virginia could have said, You took the very words out of my mouth. Instead, she murmured, 'I hope it won't come to that.'

'It had better not,' he assured her. 'A house without a kitchen simply isn't operational.'

'I agree,' she replied, 'but some things are beyond my control. Repairing this floor happens to be one of them.'

'I'm willing to pay your crew overtime, if need be.'

'There are still only twenty-four hours in a day. Nothing you're prepared to pay is going to alter that.'

'No,' Jordan Caine agreed thoughtfully. 'I don't suppose it is.'

His surprisingly mild response encouraged Virginia to voice yet another unsolicited opinion, one that, if he chose to acknowledge it, might also satisfy her curiosity about the absent Mrs Caine. 'You know,' she said, 'it might not be such a bad idea if the kitchen is delayed until your wife gets here. Most women consider it to be the focal point of the whole house and like to have some say in its design.'

His expression could not have closed more firmly had it been a door slammed shut in a driving wind. 'I do not have a wife,' he said with a finality that pre-empted any possibility of further elaboration.

'I see,' Virginia said, not seeing at all. Was he divorced, widowed, or had he never been married to begin with?

'I suppose we could eat out if we have to,' he went on, 'but I'd really prefer not to. My son... his life has been disrupted for too long. I'd like him to feel he's finally found a permanent home.'

There was such a look of desolation about Jordan Caine at that moment that Virginia's heart went out to him. His life, too, she surmised, had seen its share of upheaval. 'I'll do my very best to have things ready,' she promised.

He looked at her consideringly. 'Tell you what,' he finally suggested, 'if you find yourself really pressed for time, leave the master suite till later. I can bunk down in one of the other rooms for now.'

She heaved a quiet breath of relief. 'Thank you. Given that, I'm sure we'll manage to put the rest together before you move in on Monday.'

Her assurance, however, turned out to be as premature as her relief. It was not until eleven o'clock on Saturday night that everything was ready—everything, that was, except for the room which the new master of the house would be occupying. But Virginia, taking stock of her exhausted crew, hadn't the heart or nerve to suggest they show up for work the next day. They'd already put in more hours than she'd had any right to expect, and deserved at least one day off before beginning the next stage of the project.

Instead, she came back alone on the Sunday to prepare a small bedroom overlooking the rose garden at the front of the house for Jordan Caine's temporary occupancy. Its floor had been completely covered by carpet, so the hardwood underneath would require little more than cleaning and waxing, but the dull and faded colour of the walls convinced her that the fastest route to a spanking fresh look was to slap on a new coat of paint.

Of course, it took two coats. And of course, the stepladder was barely high enough for her to reach the ten-foot-high ceiling, but these were the sort of minor irritations she was used to and counted for nothing beside the satisfaction of having the first part of her contract completed on time.

She had half a wall still to go when she heard the back door open just before five in the afternoon. 'You're early,' she called out, assuming it was Susan, who'd promised to come over with David and bring a picnic supper. Virginia didn't know how she'd manage without Susan, who oversaw the smooth running of their home, helped David with his business, and was a good friend to boot. 'Give me another ten minutes, and I'll be down.'

Virginia realized her mistake when Jordan Caine appeared in the doorway. 'Good God, woman!' he exclaimed, eyeing the step ladder and assorted clutter. 'What in the world do you think you're doing?'

'Painting your room,' she replied, too surprised to see him to consider the wisdom of her words. 'What does it look like?'

'As if you're part of the décor,' he said, inspecting her from head to toe and leaving her supremely conscious that she was hardly dressed in her Sunday best. 'I'd even go so far as to say there's more paint on you than there is on the walls. Why didn't you delegate a couple of your crew for the job?'

'Because they have the right to relax and spend some time with their families,' she said, 'and if the last three weeks have been any indication, they won't be doing much of either until your house is finished. In view of that, I gave them today off.'

'I see.' He looked around at the paint cans and rollers in the middle of the floor, at the electric floor polisher and vacuum cleaner parked in one corner. 'And what about you? Don't you deserve a break, too?'

'The boss never takes time off until the job is done. That's part of my work ethic.'

'Is that a fact?' He shucked off his lightweight jacket and slung it on the door handle. 'In that case, you'd better put me to work, since *I'm* the boss.'

'What?'

'Put me to work,' he repeated. 'What do you want me to do? Finish the painting? Clean up the mess you've made? Vacuum under the bed?'

'Vacuum? You?' On the brink of gaping, she caught herself just in time. 'Don't make me laugh!'

He almost smiled with real amusement for the second time in their acquaintance and rolled up the sleeves of his expensive, custom-made shirt. She might have known his arms would be all smooth tanned muscle underneath but what she couldn't quite believe was that he was proposing to shed his lordly attitude and help her clean up his room.

'Would you prefer I use the broom you swooped in on instead, Virginia?' he asked drily.

'I'd prefer to be left alone to finish what I started, Mr Caine,' she said. The room was too small for his overpowering presence and she...goodnight, she was overcome by a self-conscious awareness that left her all thumbs and stammering blushes! What was the matter with her?

'I didn't offer you that choice,' he said. 'Furthermore, I thought we'd progressed beyond the ''Mr Caine-Miss Kent'' stage. I prefer to call you Virginia and, since we're going to be working so closely together, you may call me Jordan.'

'What if I prefer to call you Joey?'' she enquired, not sure which of them she was trying to impress with her audacity.

'I didn't offer you that choice, either, Virginia,' he warned, and extended an imperious hand to help her off the step ladder.

She looked at the contoured strength of his forearm, at the intense blue of his heavily lashed eyes, at the passionate curve of his beautifully fashioned mouth. And shimmied up another rung on the ladder as if he were the original serpent from the Garden of Eden. 'I'm not quite finished up here,' she insisted, chagrined at the breathless flutter in her voice.

He sighed in feigned annoyance. 'Oh, yes, you are,' he declared and, ignoring her startled squeak, swept an arm around her waist and deposited her on the floor. 'Give me the roller,' he said calmly. 'I'll finish the wall while you take the dust sheets off the furniture. If we work as a team, it'll all be finished within a couple of hours and we can both enjoy the rest of the evening off.'

'You'll get paint all over your good clothes,' she protested.

He spared her a mocking glance. 'No, I won't. That's your forte, not mine.'

'These aren't my good clothes,' she argued, tugging David's paint-spattered old shirt down around her knees and wishing she'd worn something other than a pair of ratty tennis shorts underneath it.

'Good God, I should hope not,' he said, laughing. 'Stop scowling, Virginia, you'll give yourself wrinkles before your time.'

It would take sharper wits than she seemed to possess to win a verbal skirmish with him, and the insight of a genius to figure out what made him tick. 'I'm going down to get the Murphy's Oil,' she muttered, ungraciously conceding defeat on both scores. 'This floor needs a good cleaning before we do anything else. The furniture can wait until later.'

He had to admit she'd surprised him. He'd never thought to see the day when he'd come across Virginia Mary Alexandra Kent perched atop a step-ladder, looking more like a ragged urchin than the lady of the manor.

On the other hand, 'urchin' conjured up images of bony knees and underfed frames, and there was nothing of either about Virginia Mary Alexandra. Her knees were as sweetly smooth and delicate as a baby's, and her frame...

Jordan blinked and wielded the paint-laden roller with energy. Her frame, he rebuked himself, didn't bear dwelling on if he seriously intended to carry through with his original plan—and was none of his business no matter what he intended. He certainly wasn't about to let a winsome smile and alluring body make him forget that, underneath all that delightfully feminine demeanour, Kent blood ran in her veins and Kent upbringing had shaped her character. That he would consider, even for a moment, entering into anything other than a strictly business relationship with her made him little better than the man he despised more than anyone else on earth.

And yet... Ignoring his recent advice to her, he scowled ferociously at his handiwork. Was it fair to inflict the sins of the father on the children? Hadn't he risen far enough on his own merit that he could afford to go forward instead of harking back to old injuries and insults?

Her laughter, musical and sweet like her voice, echoed up the stairs. 'Susan! I didn't hear you come in. Where's David?'

David. The younger brother. Jordan remembered him, too. Tall for his age, even at four, and as profoundly handsome as she had been beautiful, but quiet and studious where she'd been vivacious and light-hearted.

Another voice, lower, subdued, answered her, and a minute later Virginia came running back upstairs. 'I have to go,' she panted, stopping briefly in the doorway. 'My brother's dog got loose somehow.'

'What about this job you were supposed to finish?' he enquired shortly.

She flapped one of her dainty little hands at him, as if he'd asked the most boorish question imaginable. 'This is more important,' she said. 'Sorry.'

And before he could refute her statement, she was gone, flying down the stairs again, light as a dancer. Unwillingly, he found himself drawn to the window, saw her rush through the front door, climb into her jazzy little two-seater, and race off down the driveway without so much as a backward glance.

'You seem to have forgotten who's calling the shots, Virginia,' he murmured, as she swished through the gates and swung left down the hill toward the lakefront. 'I can see I'm going to have to make a point of reminding you.'

CHAPTER THREE

IT WASN'T Lucas who'd run off, Virginia discovered when she arrived home. It was one of the pups he'd sired, a year-old male they'd named Tramp with whom David had just begun working in the expectation that, when the dog matured, he would graduate as a seeing-eye companion.

Virginia recognized at once that David was frantic, even though all he said was, 'Damn!' in that quiet, controlled way that had become his trademark since the accident.

'He can't have gone far, David. We'll find him,' she said consolingly.

'But he's still a pup with no more traffic sense than a two-year-old child,' David said. 'If he gets as far as the main road...'

'He won't,' Virginia insisted with more optimism than certainty. 'Susan's driving the Jeep and has taken the short cut over the fields. She'll cut him off at the cross roads if he went that way. But it's much more likely that he headed straight for the lake. It's where you always take him for his evening walk, David, and, except for the kennel compound, it's the place he knows best. I'll ride down there on my bike and take a look. You stay here in case he shows up. And try not to worry. He'll be fine, you'll see.'

She prayed she was right, and was dreadfully afraid she was wrong when she reached the end of the narrow gravel path that ended at the lake and saw that the shore was deserted in both directions. When combing the surrounding area didn't turn up any sign of Tramp either, she had no choice but to return home.

By then, daylight had all but gone. The spot where the Jeep was usually parked stood empty, which had to mean that Susan was still out searching the main road into town. Dreading having to face David without better news, Virginia decided to pedal up the hill which wound away from the lake and toward the mansion. The hedge-rows lining both sides were probably full of intoxicating scents for a dog with a nose like Tramp's, and might have been what tempted him to choose that route over the other two.

She was rounding the third corner when she heard the sound of a car approaching too fast from the opposite direction. A second later, she found herself dazzled by its headlights. In an attempt to veer to the side, she turned her front wheel too sharply and succeeded only in coming to such an abrupt stop that she fell off the bike altogether.

Brakes squealed and a door slammed. Irate footsteps covered the few yards that separated her from the front fender of the car. A hand grabbed her by the scruff of the neck as though its bearer intended to shake her. The collar of her paint shirt snapped tight against her throat and trapped the hair hanging loose at her nape.

'You prize idiot!' Jordan Caine roared, yanking her upright. 'What the hell do you think you're doing, drifting all over the place like that? Haven't you ever heard of keeping clear of oncoming traffic? Or do you think you own the whole bloody road?'

'You were exceeding the posted speed limit,' Virginia yelled back, too unnerved to care that she was screeching like a fishwife. 'Or can't you read well enough to under-stand it?'

He did shake her then. Not hard, not violently, but in the exasperated way a parent might try to impress some sense on a wilful and unreasonable child. 'Be very grateful that my car's brakes work as well as they do or you might not be alive to make a remark like that, Virginia. And just for the record, I was travelling well within the speed limit, though you can be forgiven for claiming otherwise since, if your departure from my house earlier was any indication, you drive like a bat out of hell yourself.'

If his self-command was impressive, his condescension was infuriating. 'Let go of me,' she seethed.

He complied with an alacrity that suggested he'd found touching her thoroughly repulsive to begin with. 'Gladly. In fact, if you'll move that thing——' he pointed disdainfully at her magenta mountain bike '—I'll be on my way and spare both of us the annoyance of having to put up with each other's company a minute longer.'

She would have liked to tell him to move his car instead, except that he'd undoubtedly have done so—by driving right over her bike, which lay with its wheels still spinning in the middle of the road. Stooping, she set it upright again and pushed it over to the grass verge, glad to see Jordan Caine slide back into his driver's seat and engage the gear shift in his car. If nothing else, she'd soon be rid of his presence.

But he hadn't quite finished with her. 'By the way,' he called out, lowering the window and cruising to a stop next to her, 'did you find the missing dog?'

'No, and I'm never likely to if I keep running into people like you.'

He stared through the windshield and whistled tunelessly for a second, then sighed and shook his head before casting a weary eye her way. 'You really don't deserve to be told this,' he remarked, in a voice that suggested he was earning Brownie points with the angels for his patience and forbearance, 'but I saw something trotting along the ditch about a hundred yards back. It looked a bit like a wolf. Had eyes that glowed green in the reflection of the car lights, and ears like radar traps.'

The words galvanized her with hope. 'Well, why on earth didn't you say so before now?'

'Forgive me. I was more concerned with making sure Little Red Riding Hood hadn't scraped her knees when she fell off her bike than I was in verifying the identity of Grandmama. I suppose you expect me to turn around and drive you back up the hill so that——?'

'No, thanks. Tramp wouldn't be seen dead riding in a car like yours,' she retorted, and wondered if Jordan's particular brand of rudeness was catching because, to her certain knowledge, she'd never before spoken to anyone with such discourtesy.

'If he learned road sense from you, he isn't likely to be seen alive, either, unless you corral him fast. Sure you don't want to hitch a ride back with me?'

She was sorely tempted. So much so that she'd opened her mouth to accept when, in the red glow of the Lincoln's rear brake lights, she saw Tramp loping back down the hill toward her. 'Quite sure,' she said.

Jordan hesitated a moment, then shrugged. 'Suit yourself.'

The car started to roll slowly down the hill. From the open window, his voice once more floated out into the night. 'Better not be late for work in the morning, Virginia. You left before you'd finished what you started and the moving van will be at the house by eleven.'

He cruised another five yards or so. 'Oh, and you might consider getting yourself a set of training wheels until you learn to ride your bike properly,' he taunted, then stepped on the accelerator and disappeared round the curve in a swish of power.

'Jackass!' she muttered, and winced at yet another unladylike addition to her vocabulary inspired by the infuriating Jordan Caine.

She was at the mansion by eight the next morning, determined to make her client's temporary quarters habitable and allow him no further cause for comment or complaint. But he'd outsmarted her yet again. The room, she discovered, was already finished—by him, no doubt, the evening before, which probably explained what had kept him there so long after she'd left. No sign remained of paint-pot or step-ladder. The floor gleamed, the windows sparkled.

If it had been anyone else, she'd have been grateful for the time saved which allowed her the chance to make a last-minute tour of the other rooms. But she didn't want to feel indebted to Jordan Caine; favours from him, freely given or otherwise, sat uncomfortably, a leaden lump that sooner or later would, she knew, cause her severe indigestion.

Shortly after ten, voices in the garden below Maria Caine's sitting-room warned Virginia that the new residents had arrived. Peeping over the wrought-iron railing on the balcony, she saw Maria leading a delicate dark-haired child by the hand.

'So much garden for one little boy!' Maria exclaimed. 'It is bigger than a park, Patrick.'

'Just like Grandmother Winslow's garden,' the child replied, seeming not nearly as impressed by the grandeur as Maria. 'It's lonely.'

'Lonely?' Maria swept the child to her side in a hug. 'How can it be lonely when you have me and your papa to play with? Or do you think I'm too old to catch a ball?'

The child shook his head doubtfully. 'But we won't be allowed to play on the grass, Grandmother Caine. It's one of the rules.'

'Whose rules?' Maria snorted. 'And who told you to call me Grandmother Caine as if I were a queen or something? We will play on the grass any time we feel like it, my little one, and you will call me Nonna. Now come into the house and let's see where we're going to live...'

Their voices died away, drowned out by birdsong, but Virginia remained on the balcony, gripped by an inexplicable melancholy at what she'd witnessed. That child, that fragile, uncertain little boy, was like a shadow wandering through a cold, unwelcoming world. Where was the joy, the excitement, with which he ought to have greeted his new home? What sort of life had he known that he expected so little instead of so much?

'...And this, if I'm not lost already, is where I'll sleep. See, there's a little sitting-room as well, where we can visit by ourselves sometimes and tell each other secrets.'

Virginia stepped quickly inside the balcony door as Maria Caine entered the suite from the opposite end. 'Hello, Mrs Caine. I hope I didn't startle you. I was checking to make sure everything's ready for you.'

'Oh!' Hands clasped under her chin, Jordan's mother gazed around and exclaimed with pleasure at the flowered chintz draperies and soft peach carpet whose tone was echoed in the pale wash of colour on the walls 'Oh, Virginia, how pretty you have made it! How did you know what I would like when I didn't know myself! Never did I have such colours! Always, we were sensible, you know? Browns and grays, they don't show the wear and tear.'

'I'm glad you like it. Welcome home, Mrs Caine.'

'Have you forgotten?' Maria scolded. 'If you call me "Mrs Caine", then I shall have to call you "Miss Kent", and that is much too stiff between good friends.'

'I think Mr Caine would prefer to keep our association confined to business,' Virginia murmured, trying to be diplomatic.

'My son chooses his friends without asking me what I think,' Maria replied staunchly, 'and I will do the same. Just because we all sleep under the same roof again, that doesn't mean that he tells me how to live my life. So, what's it to be? Mrs Caine, or my friend Maria?'

Jordan would have her head for it, but suddenly Virginia didn't care. 'My friend Maria,' she agreed, and wondered how so warm and affable a lady had managed to produce such a sour son.

Maria nodded, satisfied. 'Good. Now I must introduce someone. Virginia, this is Patrick, my grandson.'

The boy stepped forward like a well-trained animated wooden soldier. 'How do you do?' he piped gravely.

'Hello.' Virginia took the small, spotlessly clean hand he extended and shook it solemnly. 'I'm very pleased to meet you at last, Patrick. I've wondered what you're like ever since I started preparing your room for you.'

Patrick looked around his grandmother's sitting-room. 'Is it the same as this?' he enquired apprehensively.

'Not at all! It's got lots of bright colours and space to set up toy trains and things. But instead of telling you about it, why don't I show it to you? Then, if there's something you think you'd like to change, we can talk about it and see what can be done. It's just down the hall from here.'

'Will my nanny's room be next door?' Patrick asked, dragging his heels as the distance between his room and Maria's lengthened.

'Nanny's room?' Alarmed that some awful oversight had occurred, Virginia looked to Maria for clarification. 'I didn't realize . . .'

'You're a big boy now. You don't need a nanny,' Maria said.

'But I always have my nanny. Grandmother Winslow says all little gentlemen have nannies until they go away to school.' Patrick regarded Maria from large, fearful brown eyes. 'Am I going to be sent away to school now that I don't live with Grandmother Winslow any more?'

'Never,' Maria announced positively. 'Five years I have waited to get to know my only grandson. Do you think I would let you leave me so soon?'

The child almost wilted with relief until a new fear assailed him. 'But if I have a bad dream, who will hear me, Grandmother Caine?'

'I will. I shall sleep with one ear open. And if I forget and leave it closed, you will come to my room and climb into bed with me until the bad dream goes away. Now, Virginia, it is time we saw this big boy's room, don't you think?'

Nervously, Virginia opened the door to his room, increasingly aware that Jordan's son was not an average five-year-old. That chilling lack of excitement and disturbing air of repressed anxiety had no place in a happy child's life.

'It's big,' Patrick said, stopping short in the doorway. 'It's lonely.'

Over his head, Maria exchanged glances with Virginia. 'It is wonderful! Your papa would have given anything to have such a room when he was your age.'

'I don't like it.'

It was a plea for familiarity, Virginia realized, rather than a rejection of her taste. Dropping to her knees, she said, 'It'll look different when the furniture gets here. You've got a bright red bed that looks like a fire truck, with a big toy box under the hood.'

'I don't want a fire truck, I want my teddy bears,' Patrick said, tears trembling in his voice. 'They were all over my wall at Grandmother Winslow's house.'

'You live here now, not at Grandmother Winslow's.' Jordan Caine's voice whipped into the room like a blast of cold air.

Three pairs of startled eyes swung around to find him filling the doorway. 'Go softly, Joey,' Maria cautioned. 'It is all strange for him and he is doing the best he can.'

'Then he'll have to do better. He should have been weaned from teddy bears years ago.'

Virginia turned away. She couldn't stand to see the expression in Jordan's eyes when he looked at his son. 'If you'll excuse me,' she murmured, attempting to slide out of the room discreetly.

'Stay where you are,' Jordan commanded. 'The furniture you ordered to go in here just arrived. They'll be bringing it upstairs any minute and you'll have to direct them where to put it. As for you, Patrick, not only will you live with the room the way it is, you'll learn to like it, too. So don't let me hear any more whining about teddy bears.'

'Joey!' Maria protested.

He turned a forbidding eye her way. 'Momma, please take him downstairs so that he isn't underfoot while the furniture is being arranged.'

The silence left behind when Maria did as he requested fairly screamed with tension. Jordan paced to the window and stared moodily out. Virginia watched and waited, full of pity for the child and anger for the father.

At length, Jordan spoke. 'Well, why don't you say it?'

'Say what?'

'That I'm an unfeeling, miserable excuse for a father. That it's a pity they don't make training wheels for parents, because I sure as hell could use a set. That you wouldn't wish me on Lizzie Borden, let alone an innocent child like Patrick.'

'If you already know all that, there's not much use in my repeating it, is there, Mr Caine?'

'Don't use that uppity tone with me, Virginia.' He spun around to face her. 'Your own father wasn't exactly perfect, in case you've forgotten.'

There it was again, that reference to her family that indicated Jordan shared some sort of past with her. 'My father was never cruel to my brother or me when we were little,' she said, deeming it not the right time to delve into the mystery. 'He never once spoke to us the way you just spoke to your son.'

'No, he reserved that tone for other people.'

'Even if he did, that doesn't excuse your behaviour. Patrick is just a little boy. He's obviously homesick and scared. And his father, the one person he ought to be able to count on to make everything seem better, treated him as if he were some sort of outcast. If you have so little feeling for him, why didn't you leave him with his other grandmother?'

'Because I want him to grow up to be a man, not some effete and pampered mama's boy. And because he's a Caine, not a Winslow.'

'Oh, give me strength!' Virginia laughed scornfully. 'Are you afraid having a sensitive little boy like Patrick for a son might cast doubts on your virility? I'd never have guessed you were so insecure.'

'I've told you before not to push your luck, Virginia,' Jordan cautioned, striding across to where she stood and spinning her around. 'And if it's proof of my virility you want, then it can certainly be arranged, beginning right now.'

The power in his grip gentled as he slid his hands from her shoulders to her throat. To her alarm, Virginia experienced a corresponding softening deep inside, as if he'd brushed her intimately with a lover's touch. 'Oh, my,' she said on a nervously abbreviated breath, 'you're going to flex your manly muscles and I'm supposed to go all weak-kneed with the thrill of it and admit that yes, yes, you truly are a powerhouse of passion barely contained within the human form.'

His eyes sparked blue fury. 'You snotty little witch, you still think you're too good for the likes of me, don't you?'

'Yes,' she said, not sure what he meant by 'still' and not particularly caring to find out at that moment. It was more important that he not discover the disgraceful tide of sexual excitement rushing through her blood. 'I never did care for apes, nor have I had occasion to deal with one since I left my teens behind. The men I know outgrew that sort of thing a long time ago.'

The fire in his eyes subsided to a smoulder. 'Then it's time someone showed you how the other half lives, Virginia,' he said with menacing softness. 'And if the flush on your cheeks is anything to go by, you can hardly wait to find out.'

His mouth, which so often appeared hard and unsmiling, descended on hers like a tropical breeze. Strong enough to have her bending to its will, gentle enough to vanquish her outrage, and just hot enough to melt her resistance.

She bloomed beneath it, a wild, uncontrolled flowering of desire as shocking as it was unexpected. Her eyes fell shut, her knees sagged, and she fumbled for the lapels of his jacket to keep herself upright. Her lips parted in brazen invitation.

And he declined to accept. 'Well, well,' he drawled, 'I guess we both just learned something, didn't we?'

Her eyes flew open to find him staring down at her mockingly. 'Did we?' she gasped, light-headed and breathless as her heart continued to pummel at her ribs.

He smiled, wicked delight curving his lips in a parenthesis of glee. 'Of course we did, Virginia. You were expecting me to throw you over my shoulder and carry you off to my lair with the intention of having my clumsy, loutish way with you. And I discovered you were more than willing to let me.'

'And then I slapped him. Across the face.' Virginia put down her fork, afraid she'd gag on the chicken Neptune Susan had prepared for dinner that evening.

David sipped his wine calmly. 'Hard, I hope.'

'I'm afraid so. It sounded like a rifle shot ricocheting off the walls. I'm sure the moving men must have heard and wondered what it was. And when I looked at him, the mark of my fingers was imprinted across his cheek.' Propping one elbow on the table, she sank her forehead against her hand. 'I've never been so ashamed or horrified in my life.'

Wide-eyed with curiosity, Susan put down her wine glass and leaned forward. 'What did he do?'

'He raised his eyebrows and shook his head. "Princesses aren't supposed to do things like that, Virginia," he said. "I'm no princess," I told him, whereupon he looked at me as if I'd just crawled out of the gutter and said, "You're no lady, either."' Her voice quavered with chagrin. 'And the worst of it is, he's right. About everything.'

'Oh, dear.' David smiled broadly. 'Do I take that to mean you enjoyed being kissed by His Horribleness?'

She blushed furiously. 'It's not funny! I thought I'd be repelled.'

'Why? As I recall, you said he was quite handsome.'

'Yes, I did.' But the description didn't exactly do Jordan Caine justice any more. It was too bland.

'Do you think he'll fire you?'

'No—at least, not right away, because his parting words were for me to bring the sketches and notes I've made for the rest of the house when I show up tomorrow.'

'In that case,' David said, 'I think I'll drop by and pay my respects. I'm rather curious to meet the man who's got you so rattled.'

'Oh, you'll probably bring out his best side and wonder what I'm making so much fuss about,' Virginia decided gloomily. 'I bet he doesn't put a foot wrong with you.'

'The kitchen is a dream, Joey! I could spend the rest of my life in here and never grow tired of it.'

'You won't get the chance. I'm hiring a cook, Momma. Just because you got your own way about making breakfast this morning, it doesn't mean it's a permanent arrangement. Your kitchen days are numbered.'

'Don't be foolish. How am I to keep myself occupied?'

'Invite your friends over to visit. Have your chauffeur bring the car and take you for a ride downtown. Start making a guest list for the Miners' Ball. Go shopping for a gown.'

'Those are not the things that make life full and interesting for a woman like me—except, perhaps, for the part about my friends.' His mother stroked the dark green marble counter-tops lovingly and patted the gleaming Lavazza coffee maker specially imported from Italy. 'Making a home and being a mother is what I'm good at, Joey.'

'Learn to be a full time grandmother and get to know your grandson.'

'As if there is any question that I wouldn't!' She shot a sly glance his way that he wasn't supposed to notice. 'But an old lady like me doesn't take a father's place and Patrick is smart enough to know that.'

Jordan scowled and made a big production of loading his coffee cup into the dishwasher. 'I don't have a lot of time to spend with him right now.'

'You didn't have time when your daughter was born, either, my son, until it was too late.'

Remarks like that made Jordan question the wisdom of bringing his mother to live here. He didn't need daily reminders of his failures, particularly not by someone who didn't know the whole story. Yet to tell her what it had been like during those last months before his wife and their infant daughter had been killed would break his mother's heart more thoroughly than either of them could bear.

'Patrick doesn't seem to mind not being around me,' he said defensively. 'Anyone would think I'm in the habit of beating him, the way he cowers whenever he sees me.'

'He is afraid of you. He thinks you don't like him.' Maria shrugged her plump shoulders. 'The way you look at him sometimes, I think you don't like him, too.'

'That's absurd! He's my son, and of course I don't dislike him. But I don't pretend to understand him, either.' Which was an understatement to put it mildly, since he was, in fact, terrified of the boy.

'What don't you understand? That he is different from you?'

... are you afraid he might cast a doubt on your virility... ? I'd never have guessed you were so insecure.

The voice, the musical fall of derisive laughter like crystal bells chiming in the breeze, rang again in Jordan's head. Her face swam into focus, the beautiful gray eyes haughty with contempt then, moments later, melting and closing as her lips rose to meet his.

Suddenly he could taste her again, her achingly sweet mouth eclipsing the lingering fragrance of coffee. The same rush of desire that had laid seige to him yesterday threatened anew, less savage but no less infuriating. If he'd thought to prove his dominance with that incongruous kiss, her imperious little hand had swiftly reminded him that, reversed fortunes notwithstanding, he was still the stable boy and she still the princess.

Jordan clenched an impotent fist and swung around to face his mother again. 'I've got to get going. I'll be in the library interviewing applicants for the position of mine manager for the next hour or so but if Virginia Kent shows up in the meantime, tell her not to go traipsing off somewhere else. I've got a few things to sort out with her first.'

'You speak Virginia's name and your eyes grow full of fire. Why does the thought of her make you angry? She has done nothing but make things pleasant for us here.'

'That's what she's being paid to do, Momma. And though she seems inclined to forget that, I am not.'

'Perhaps it was a mistake to hire her at all if it stirs up so much resentment in you. There's no changing the past, my son, and you would be a more contented man if you could forget it.'

'I don't want to forget it. And I don't intend for her to, either.'

'But she is not the one guilty of any sin. She should not have to suffer.'

'Nor was my father,' Jordan reminded her grimly, 'yet he paid with his life anyway.'

CHAPTER FOUR

ONCE again, Jordan Caine kept Virginia cooling her heels in the hall outside the library while he dealt with more important matters within.

Maria found her there. 'But this is good,' she exclaimed, overcoming Virginia's objections and ushering her to the kitchen at the back of the house, 'because now we can have another little visit.'

'That won't go down too well with the boss if he finds out,' Virginia said, though she was fast approaching the point where she didn't give a rap how the boss felt.

'How can he object, if we confine ourselves to business?' Maria shrugged, turning her attention to an electric coffee-maker that would have looked perfectly at home in one of the trendy cappuccino bars down on Grand Avenue. Not the least bit fazed by its complicated operation, she poured beans into a funnel, twiddled levers, turned knobs and steamed milk without once missing a beat in the conversation. 'We shall sit in the sun and enjoy our coffee while you tell me the wonderful plans you have for the rest of this old house. That way, you will have a clear conscience and I shall have the pleasure of your company.'

Outside the breakfast-room, a raised cedar deck holding a small wrought-iron table and four chairs overlooked the rest of the house and part of the pool area. Pink rambler roses climbed over the brick wall surrounding the vegetable garden. Far below, at the bottom of the hill, Opal Lake lived up to its name, shimmering aquamarine and emerald and sapphire beneath a cloudless sky.

Allowing Virginia to carry the tray, Maria settled into one of the chairs and fanned herself with a dish towel.

'Tell me, *cara*,' she sighed, her gaze fixed on the pan-
orama spread out below, 'do you think so much beauty
outside and all the lovely things you plan for inside will
bring contentment to those now living in this house?'

The question cast a shadow over the brightness of the
day for Virginia, reviving memories best forgotten. She
knew better than anyone that no amount of window-
dressing could fill a home with happiness if what lay
underneath was empty of love and rotten with deceit. 'I
think contentment has to come from within a person,
Maria.'

'I wish you would explain that to my son.'

'I doubt he'd listen. He strikes me as very...' She pulled
fabric samples from her briefcase and spread them on
the table while she searched for a tactful word to describe her client. When 'pigheaded' was the best she
could drum up, she decided that silence was the better
part of discretion.

'If you are thinking "stubborn",' Maria said with a
smile, 'you are right. He has been that way since he was
a little boy.'

Privately, Virginia had the utmost difficulty imagining Jordan as anything other than the full-grown,
autocratic man he was today, but that was another ob-
servation she didn't feel entitled to pass on to his mother.
'He's certainly very determined that the house is going
to be finished and ready for the Midsummer Miners'
Festival, which reminds me that I wanted to ask what
you think of balloon shades for the drawing-room
windows?' She selected a couple of swatches of fabric
and offered them for Maria's inspection. 'Either in this
satin brocade, or the silk moiré?'

'I think you don't want my opinion on silks and satins
so much as you don't want to offer yours on my son,
cara.'

Virginia was spared having to field that astute remark
by Patrick's sudden appearance at the foot of the steps
leading from the garden to the deck. 'There's a man

walking to the house,' he said timidly. 'He's got a big dog.'

David! Virginia thought, remembering that her brother had said he'd drop by some time today. Rising, she asked, 'Where exactly is he, Patrick?'

'Round near the front door. He wanted to talk to me, but I ran away because his dog might bite me.'

'Ah, *nipote*!' Maria scolded, struggling to her feet also. 'You must learn not to be so rude. First, you tell Virginia you don't like the room she prepared for you, now you run and hide from visitors.'

'This particular visitor won't have noticed,' Virginia started to explain, when David himself, tall, blond and elegantly handsome in pearl-gray slacks and an open-necked white shirt, rounded the corner of the house.

'I came to welcome you to the neighborhood and followed the voices,' he said, smiling. 'I hope you don't mind?'

Virginia saw the flash of comprehension in Maria's expression and knew that David heard the compassion that softened her thick Italian accent when she replied, 'We are honoured, *signore*.'

'Here, David.' Virginia guided him up the steps and waited until he found the chair Maria pulled out for him before continuing, 'This is my brother David, Maria. I don't know if you're aware of it but, even though we live at the bottom of the hill, we're still your closest neighbors.'

Maria made a valiant effort to hide her distress. 'That is wonderful. You will join us for coffee, Signor David, please?'

'How can I say no?' He bathed Maria in his dear, sweet smile. 'I could smell it the minute I set foot inside the garden. Brazilian dark roast, isn't it?'

'*Si—tostarlo nero*. I will make some fresh especially for you.' Her voice trembled with emotion and she looked away, searching for a scapegoat on which to defuse it. Her glance fell on Patrick, who'd taken refuge on the far side of the table. 'But first, there is a young rascal here who ran away from you in the garden, and I think he would like to say something about that, yes, Patrick?'

Patrick slithered behind the safety of the remaining chair and eyed Lucas warily. 'Does your dog bite?' he asked.

'No,' David said, reaching down to lay his hand lovingly on Lucas's noble head. 'He's very well-mannered.'

'Unlike you,' Maria informed her grandson severely. 'Those are not the words I wanted to hear. At the very least, say hello to our guest.'

'How do you do?' Patrick parroted absently, his gaze still glued on Lucas. 'What's that thing on his back?'

'It's a harness that I hold when we're out walking.'

'Why does he have to wear it if he doesn't bite people?'

'It makes it easier for me to follow him, and it also tells him that he's on duty. He's a seeing-eye dog.'

Patrick digested that bit of news along with a cookie from the plate Maria had set on the table, then admitted, 'I don't know what that means.'

'I can't see,' David explained, 'so Lucas sees for me.'

'How come you can't see? Don't your eyes work?' Patrick asked, and Virginia thought Maria was going to faint.

'Not any more. They were badly burned in an accident when I was in high school and I've been blind ever since.'

'He is full of questions today,' Maria interjected apologetically. '*Nipote*, take your cookie and play in the garden while the grown-ups visit and have their coffee.'

But Patrick found David much more interesting than anything the garden had to offer. 'Did you get caught in a fire?' he persisted.

'Patrick!' Maria shooed at him with her apron. 'Enough of the questions for today.'

'That's all right, Maria. It's natural for him to be curious,' David said and turned back to the child. 'I was burned by chemicals during an experiment in the school lab. A test tube exploded and splashed its contents in my eyes.'

'Did it hurt?'

'Yes, very much.'

'Did you go to the hospital?'

'Yes.'

'Did you have an operation?'

'Yes. More than one.'

'That means you got a scar.' Patrick gazed in awe. 'Can I see it?'

Maria let out a little squeak of dismay, but David smiled again and removed his dark glasses. 'There's nothing to see.'

'Oh, well...' Disappointed at the outcome of that topic, Patrick's interest returned to Lucas. 'Are you sure your dog doesn't bite?'

'Quite sure. Would you like to stroke him?'

Patrick's eyes grew round. 'Does he have big teeth?'

'Very. But he won't let you see them.'

'Grandmother Winslow had a little white dog. It used to bite. The gardener said it was a nippy little bugger and I should leave it alone.'

Maria squeaked again and covered her face with the dish towel. Somewhere inside the house, a telephone rang.

'Lucas would be embarrassed to behave like that,' David assured the boy.

'Well...' Clearly tempted, Patrick edged a little closer. 'Maybe...'

'Let me unhitch his harness first,' David suggested, 'then just hold out your hand, like this, and let him sniff you.'

Virginia suspected that what followed was probably the most courageous thing Patrick had done in his short, sheltered little life. He inched forward, held out a trembling hand, squeezed his eyes shut, and hung on to his breath with all his might.

Lucas, with the impeccable manners of a pedigreed gentleman, touched his black nose slowly to the child's palm. A moment ticked by, followed by another. And then Patrick doubled up and squealed, an ear-splitting, blood-curdling screech whose echo seemed to hang in the air for ever.

The door from the house shot open and footsteps skidded to a halt on the deck. 'Oh, God!' Jordan prayed, in a low, shaken voice. 'Call off the dog!'

David took it upon himself to respond for the Almighty, then turned to Virginia and muttered, 'What's all the fuss about?'

Unfortunately, Jordan heard and pounced on the question. 'What do you mean, *what's all the fuss about*? My son just about lost his hand down that animal's throat and if you didn't see what was happening, you must be blind.'

Into the pool of heavy silence that followed, Patrick chirped, 'He tickled!'

On the point of scooping his son out of further harm's way, Jordan stopped. 'What did you say, Patrick?'

'Lucas tickled my fingers with his whiskers when he licked me,' the child squeaked, on a spate of giggles.

As they died away, the silence thundered in again to take their place, then, 'Are you telling me,' Jordan enquired in a deadly voice, 'that you pulled this outrageous stunt because the goddamned dog *licked* you?'

'Joey, we have a guest,' Maria reminded him, as Patrick slid fearfully behind her skirts.

'I noticed,' Jordan snapped, glaring at David. 'Who are you, anyway?'

'David Kent, Virginia's brother. And in response to your earlier remark, yes, as a matter of fact, I am blind, which is why I seldom go anywhere without my "goddamned dog".'

Jordan paled slightly and cleared his throat. 'I—er, didn't realize.'

'No reason that you should,' David replied equably. 'I don't hang a sign around my neck advertising the fact.'

'Maybe you ought to,' Jordan said. 'It might save people like me from shooting their mouths off.'

'I'm sorry if my dog alarmed you.'

'So am I. I just aged about forty years.'

'I was about to make more coffee, Joey,' Maria interjected a trifle anxiously. 'Will you stay and join us?'

'No, thanks.' He lifted his shoulders and grimaced. 'I just got a call from the mine. There's been another fall in one of the adits.'

'Has anyone been hurt?' David was quick to ask.

'No.' Jordan gestured at Virginia. 'Look, I hate to break up your little coffee klatch but I need to have a word with you before I go. Come to my office and bring a notepad with you.'

She swept ahead of him, stonily forestalling his attempt to hold open the library door for her. She was seething, but he appeared either unaware or uncaring of the fact.

'Have a seat,' he invited, following her into the room and flinging himself down behind the plywood contraption that still served as his desk.

'I prefer to stand,' she announced shortly. 'I don't plan to remain in your company a minute longer than I absolutely have to.'

Already scribbling notes in the margin of the paper in front of him, he looked up, weary irritation crossing his features. 'What's rattling your chain, Highness? I'm the one trying to revive a derelict mine and finding myself stymied at every turn.'

'And I'm the one whose brother you just subjected to the most appalling insensitivity without once feeling the need to mitigate your crass behaviour by so much as a word of apology or regret.'

Jordan slapped his pencil down and tilted back his chair at a dangerous angle. 'I did apologize,' he declared flatly, his eyes narrowing ominously.

'No, you did not. You brushed off your boorish behaviour as though it——'

'I apologized. I said——'

'That you hadn't realized he was blind and that it
would be a good idea if he *did* wear a sign around his
neck in the future, to warn people. David is the one who
apologized when he said that he was sorry Lucas had
alarmed you.'

The front legs of Jordan's chair slammed down on
the floor as he surged to his feet. 'Listen,' he whispered,
planting his hands flat on the plywood desk top and
leaning forward dictatorially, 'I'm sorry—*sorry*—if you
didn't like the way I reacted to your brother, but I'm
not the one who invited him or his bloody dog to come
calling, and I don't have time for the social niceties that
are the mainstay of your trite little existence.'

To her absolute chagrin, Virginia flinched a little
before his controlled rage. Even leaning over, his spine
curved with tension, he towered above her, an intimidating presence not about to give an inch.

He snatched an irate breath, then went on, his voice
rising a little with each sentence, 'There are three
thousand unemployed men in this town because previous owners of the Opal Gold Mine have been content
to milk it for easy profit to line their own pockets, then
walk away from it. There are families going to bed
hungry, and they'll continue to do so until that mine is
made safely operational again. And this morning, while
you and your brother were shooting the breeze with my
mother, a maintenance crew of twelve—husbands and
fathers, every one, Virginia—damn near lost their lives
trying to do just that. So don't expect me to get all bent
out of shape because you don't think I was *sensitive*
enough in my dealings with a man who's never in his
life known the real meaning of want or despair.'

'How do you know?' she raged back, the memory of
David's fight to come to terms with his disability vivid

in her memory. 'What makes you such an expert on me and my family?'

Jordan straightened up and looked at her from eyes as cold as Siberia in winter. 'I've seen you in action, Highness. All of you, from dear old Dad down to the butler who used to open your front door. And when it comes to insensitivity, you could write a book—but not on my time, so sit down, be quiet and listen to what I want you to tackle next, Virginia Mary Alexandra, before I lose what little patience I've got left.'

She would have liked to tell him to go to hell, because that was indubitably where he belonged. She would have relished telling him to find someone else to give orders to because she was resigning from the job. But the first simply wasn't her style, and the contract she'd signed deprived her of the luxury of the second. So, she perched on the edge of the chair facing him, her spine stiff with indignation, and favoured him with a contemptuous stare. 'This house is not the only thing requiring attention, Mr Caine. Your manners could use a little refurbishing, too. You are quite the rudest person it has ever been my misfortune to meet.'

'Then God help you when I really go on a tear—which I'm likely to do sooner rather than later if I have to put up with any more of your uninvited homilies on deportment.' He resumed his seat and picked up his pencil once more. 'So to preclude that possibility, let's get back to the business at hand. I will be issuing invitations to the Midsummer Miners' Festival and Ball at the end of the week. The date has been set for the fifth of August which, by my reckoning, leaves you nine weeks to complete your contract. I don't want any last-minute snags, Virginia, so get the word out now to your contractors and suppliers that delays won't be tolerated.'

'Aren't you being a little premature with your grandiose plans?' she enquired loftily. 'The mine isn't yet operational, let alone realizing a profit, so what's the point of reviving a tradition that, in the past, marked the celebration of a bonanza year?'

'The point is to boost morale. I want to do more than pump life into the economy of this town, I want to inject a little hope into the lives of the people who inhabit it, as well. I want the working man to know that his future lies in the hands of someone who cares about him, rather than someone whose sole aim is to get rich at his expense.'

'I'm fully aware of the commitment involved in running the only viable industry in the area, so spare me your lectures, Jordan. My grandfather and father, as you must already know, are the two men responsible for this town's even being on the map.'

'Your father damn near wiped it off the map, too. He's the one who reneged on his obligations and, when he lost interest in the family business, sold out to a someone concerned only with lining his own pockets. When was the last time you went into the mine, Virginia? Or have you ever bothered to see, first-hand, what sort of conditions men worked in down there?'

'I've seen it,' she said defensively. 'My father took me and my brother down when we were children.'

Jordan shook his head scornfully. 'Well, go down again and take a look through an adult's eyes. The place is a disaster waiting to happen and the miners know it. Yet they're prepared to risk their lives in order to make it a thriving concern again. Hosting the Festival is my way of thanking them for their support—a sort of psychological shot in the arm, if you prefer to think of it that way.'

'Well, I confess I'm surprised,' Virginia said, forced to admit that he'd taken the wind out of her sails. 'You don't strike me as the type to acknowledge the value of something as abstract as psychology.'

'Really?' A bitter smile curved his mouth. 'Then you'll probably be even more surprised to learn that I can spell the word and know it begins with ''p'', not ''s'', and that I've made extensive study of its application to industrial and employee relations. As new owner here, my obligations extend beyond making the mine a lucrative concern again. They also include looking after its personnel, not just when they're on the job but all the time. They might be blue-collar workers but that doesn't make them any less deserving of my respect and it ought to generate yours. They're the ones who made it possible for you to enjoy such luxury when you were growing up, Virginia, even if it didn't once occur to you to wonder what it cost them to provide it.'

He made her feel small and mean-spirited with that remark, but she wouldn't let him see it. 'What a pity your humanitarianism is so restricted. Or does my family's white-collar background preclude our eligibility for the same sort of consideration you're so eager to afford other people?'

'I don't owe you or your family a damn thing. You're being paid a generous fee to perform cosmetic miracles, Virginia, because it pleases me to provide an elegant home for my family, but you're about as essential to the economic health of this town as a flea—and just about as irritating.'

She shot to her feet. 'Really? Then may I assume, since you're assured your house will be ready well before August the fifth, that I'm free to remove my irritating presence?'

'Not quite,' he said, steepling his fingers and impaling her in a cool stare. 'Orchestrating the social details of the Festival, particularly the grand finale of the Miners' Ball, is no easy task. I want you to lend my mother the benefit of your experience in handling it. She has never dealt with anything on quite such a grand scale and I'm afraid she might find the whole enterprise a bit overwhelming.'

Virginia would dearly have liked to tell him that nothing in her contract required her to oblige him, but she remembered too well the time and energy her mother had devoted to the event each year. The lists of things to do, the people and services to engage, were endless, not to mention the personnel skills required to integrate the various parts into one smooth and polished whole. It was a mammoth undertaking and Virginia knew she'd never be able to abandon Maria to the clash of wills and temperament that frequently occurred between caterers and florists, hired help and resident staff.

Jordan knew it, too, and exploited her weak spot shamelessly. 'I wouldn't want her to be the target of public ridicule,' he said softly.

Sinking back into her chair, Virginia offered a last token of resistance. 'You could hire a professional party planner. Why choose me?'

'Because my mother is comfortable with you.' He almost let a smile escape but managed to retrieve it just in time. 'For some odd reason, she's fond of you and she trusts you.'

Virginia let her sigh signify assent and took small comfort in firing one last shot. 'This could have waited until another day, you know. It hardly ranks as important beside the urgency of what awaits you at the mine.'

'Unfortunately, it couldn't. I expect to be very busy for the next several weeks and might even be out of town occasionally. It's quite probable that I won't see you again until the end of July.'

Virginia was staggered by the stab of dismay that news afforded her and promptly went out of her way to disguise the fact from Jordan. 'Well, hallelujah! At least you won't be hovering over my shoulder, barking orders and generally interfering with the way things are being organized. It'll be nice to have a free hand for a change.'

He picked up several sheets of foolscap stapled together and slung them across the plywood table. 'On the contrary, Highness. Here's a long list of all the things I want to see incorporated into whatever arrangements you make.'

Virginia scanned the first page. 'Japanese lanterns strung through the trees? A country and western band at the Ball, as well as an orchestra? *Beer* alongside champagne?' She wrinkled her nose in deliberately provocative disdain. 'How... quaintly novel.'

She had hoped to goad him into reacting but she had no idea how thoroughly she'd succeed. He surged up from his seat and in one fluid movement rounded the desk and imprisoned her by the simple expedient of clamping his fists on the arms of her chair. 'You have sneered at me for the last time, Virginia,' he said, his breath fanning her face.

A wise woman would have looked away; she would have pretended confusion or apology—anything to escape the forceful proximity of a man whose horribleness never quite managed to exceed his attractiveness. But Virginia, for reasons she didn't care to examine, showed no such good sense. Instead, she stared back at him and took bold inventory of all she beheld.

He needed a haircut. His black curls were not as well tamed as they had been the day she'd come here to sign a contract. And he wasn't getting enough sleep. Those intensely blue eyes were shadowed with fatigue. His mouth was beautifully shaped and produced an alarmingly erotic response in her.

Best, after all, to look away, she conceded belatedly. And did so too late.

'Like what you see, Highness?'

The question startled her enough for her gaze to fly back to his face again, a response she promptly lived to regret. His eyes glimmered with triumphant delight. His mouth softened into a sliver of a smile, one as full of knowing amusement as his eyes, telling her he was fully aware that her heart was banging a frenzied tattoo behind her ribs. He inched closer.

'If you dare to kiss me again,' she threatened foolhardily, 'I'll——'

He kissed her. Deftly, defiantly, devastatingly. Cheekily, his tongue playing irreverent tag with hers. Lengthily and at exceeding and debilitating leisure.

She lifted her hands, intending to slap at the iron strength of his arms which continued to bar her escape, and to her horror found her fingers travelling to his shoulders and anchoring themselves briefly in the solid muscle there before sliding to his neck.

I'll bite his tongue in half, she vowed weakly. I'll teach him to take liberties with me!

And felt her mouth soften helplessly under his as a humiliating heat scorched a path down her throat to the pit of her stomach.

'You liked what you saw,' he decided with satisfaction, when at last he'd tormented her enough.

'You're a pig,' she whispered.

'Then I can only assume you harbour barnyard fantasies, my little aristocrat, because you certainly just enjoyed what this pig had to offer.'

Bad enough that she couldn't concoct a rejoinder that would annihilate him. For his contention to be right on the mark added unbearably to her misery. 'Oh,' she quavered, her eyes swimming with impotent tears, 'I hate you! I really *hate* you!'

'Yeah,' he drawled, turning his back on her. 'I know exactly how you feel.'

CHAPTER FIVE

'You did *what*?' With a clatter, Jordan dropped his linguini-laden fork to his plate, his appetite suddenly diminished.

Maria leaned over to wipe a speck of clam sauce from Patrick's chin before replying, 'I accepted an invitation for us to have dinner with Virginia and David next week.'

'When did she ask, and why would you do such a thing without consulting me first, Momma?'

'Virginia isn't the one who asked, her brother is—this morning when he stopped by to visit. You were busy going over business with her at the time and in any case, since when do I have to ask permission of my own son for something as simple and friendly as dinner with a neighbor?'

'Since you suddenly decided to take charge of my social calendar. And there's nothing friendly about these particular neighbors.'

'You're wrong, Joey. I like those young people. They aren't like their father. They're kind. And I would very much like to go and have dinner with them.'

'Then go, but don't expect to drag me along with you.'

His mother fixed him in the reproachful stare that somehow always managed to strip away the years and reduce him to the status of errant teenager again. 'Neighbors should get along. They never know when they might need one another. Have you forgotten how it was when you were a child?'

'I'll never forget,' he assured her. 'That's why I won't accept hospitality from the Kents.'

'But you must. They are being polite and repaying us for our invitation to them. Or aren't good manners important once a man becomes rich and powerful?'

61

Jordan sat up a little straighter, his attention snagged not by yet another maternal reprimand but by the information casually dropped in with it. 'What are you talking about, Momma?'

'Doing the right thing, of course. That doesn't change with the size of a man's bank account, my son, and it saddens me to think that you——'

'What invitation have we extended to them?'

'Why, to the fancy party you're planning to throw in August,' his mother replied blithely. 'I asked Signor David myself.'

Jordan groaned and dropped his forehead into his hand. 'You shouldn't have done that, Momma. Neither he nor his sister is on the guest list.'

'Well, they should be—and now they are. Take your elbows off the table, Joey, you're setting a bad example for your son.'

How Jordan contained his annoyance, he didn't know. Certainly, had it been anyone other than his mother, he would have let fly with a cutting reminder of who called the shots. But like the memories that went with them, the habits of a lifetime were not easily dismissed. 'Well, what's done is done, I suppose. Hopefully, like me, they'll choose not to accept the invitation. I'm sorry, but nothing you say will change my mind, Momma. I won't go over there for dinner.'

'Why not?' His mother looked crushed. 'Where is the harm?'

'I'm busy that night.'

'What night? We haven't set a date yet. Signor David said for us to choose an evening that is convenient.'

'There won't be one. I'll make a point of being busy, regardless.' Jordan pushed away from the table. 'Excuse me. I have a load of work to get through before tomorrow. Patrick, come and say goodnight before you go to bed.'

In passing, he reached out to ruffle his son's hair and was both irritated and saddened when the boy cringed from him. 'Why do you do that?' he snapped. 'It's not as if I've ever hit you.'

'You scare me,' Patrick whimpered. 'You shout. Grandmother Winslow says only boars shout. I'm scared of boars. I've seen pictures of them in books. They have teeth sticking out of their noses.'

It took Jordan a moment to make the connection and when he did, he had to laugh. 'She meant "boor", which is something else entirely. At least, I assume she did, since if you take a closer look, you'll see I've yet to sprout tusks from my nose. But then again, maybe she's not far wrong. Certainly, she's not the only woman who thinks I'm closely related to wild pigs.'

Ignoring his mother's gaping dismay, he looked down at his solemn-eyed son. 'You don't have to be afraid of me, Patrick. I might not be the best father in the world but I'm a long way from being the worst and I'm the only one you've got.'

Once in the sanctuary of the library, Jordan opened the bottom drawer of his metal filing cabinet and took out the bottle of Jack Daniel's he kept there. Not, he assured himself, that he was in any danger of becoming a closet alcoholic, but there were times when a man needed the solace of a quiet place and a snort of something smooth and strong to repair the ravages of the work day. Lately, he'd suffered more than his share of ravages.

The mine was a mess and it galled him beyond words that he couldn't lay the blame for that on Andrew Kent, Virginia's father. But the real culprit was Ted Connaught, Jordan's immediate predecessor. The man had cheerfully exhausted those mineral-bearing veins that were easily accessible without bothering to shore up the mine headings. And as if that wasn't bad enough, when the gold had petered out, he hadn't attempted to excavate more exploratory shafts. It had been easier to lay off his workers, cut his losses, and run. He'd been an outsider and hadn't cared that a whole town had been laid idle because of him. Trying to reverse the resulting damage was keeping Jordan awake at nights.

For that matter, so was Virginia Kent, though not in quite the same way.

He swung his feet on to the plywood table-top, crossed his ankles and tilted back the old leather desk chair that he'd bought at an auction of antique office furniture. Cradling his glass to his chest, he closed his eyes, knowing ahead of time what to expect.

She swam into his mind with the ease of a summer breeze drifting through an open window. He saw her smile, her face, her hair. He heard her voice, smelt her perfume, watched her move, the unconscious grace and elegance conferred by a privileged upbringing endowing everything about her.

Just as everything about her reduced him to a state of arousal that was downright embarrassing.

She tasted of peaches and gardenias. She felt like cream. The sweet curve of her breasts drove him to distraction and her legs should be outlawed. Her kiss tested his control more severely than rolling around in bed with any other woman ever had done, and he too often found himself thinking that he wouldn't rest until he'd made her his.

Which was usually when he reached for the Jack Daniel's. Because of all his dreams and ambitions, riding off into the sunset with Virginia Mary Alexandra Kent was pure pie-in-the-sky. No matter how impressive his corporate climb to the top, all it took was one scornful glance from those stunning gray eyes to remind him that, as far as she was concerned, he'd never amount to anyone other than the hired help.

'Papa?'

Jordan opened his eyes to find his son peeping around the door. 'Hey, son, is it bedtime already?'

Patrick nodded but made no move to come closer. Suppressing another surge of irritation, Jordan made a concerted effort to foster a more positive relationship with the boy. 'Then what do you say,' he suggested, swinging his feet to the floor, 'to my tucking you into bed for a change, instead of Nonna?'

'But she reads me a story.'

'I know how to read.'

'And kisses me goodnight.'

Jordan smothered a flash of panic and offered his hand. 'I can probably manage to do that, too.'

After a moment's dubious consideration, Patrick placed his small hand in Jordan's. 'OK.'

The boy's room was neat as a pin. A night-lamp shone from a table next to the fire engine bed where a balding stuffed teddy bear perched on the pillow. Suspended from the ceiling, a mobile of planets and stars circled slowly in the evening breeze blowing in from the lake.

Jordan felt out of place: too big, too awkward, too ignorant of small boys and their bedtime rituals. What was he supposed to do next? 'Hop in,' he invited, turning down the striped blue and red sheets.

'I have to brush my teeth and go potty first.'

'Oh, right. Do you... er, shall I wait here for you?'

The boy looked scandalized. 'You're supposed to get my toothbrush ready,' he accused.

'Yeah, right. The toothbrush.' Jordan shrugged lamely. 'Let's get on with it, then.'

The adjoining bathroom was geared for a child. Mickey Mouse cavorted on the shower curtain and adorned the rinsing mug and toothbrush holder. The toothpaste container had some sort of fancy paediatric spout, designed, Jordan presumed, eying it warily, to dispense exactly the right amount. A booster stool was parked next to the vanity.

'You need help getting up here?' he asked, toeing the stool into position.

'No,' Patrick replied scornfully, 'but you're supposed to have my toothbrush ready by now.'

Jordan brushed his own teeth at least twice a day. Had done so most of his life. But he'd forgotten how small

and delicate a child's things were in a grown man's hand.
The toothpaste shot out of the dispenser with an ener-
getic squirt that dripped off the bristles and on to the
rim of the sink.

'You made a mess,' Patrick announced smugly.
'You're not supposed——'

'I know,' Jordan replied. 'I'm not supposed to make
a mess. Well, excuse me! Here.' He placed the loaded
brush in the boy's hand and attempted to wipe up the
excess toothpaste with a tissue. A smeared and sticky
residue attested to his lack of success.

'I don't *spit* that much mess,' Patrick observed, com-
pleting his brushing and expectorating with vigour. 'Not
even down my chin.'

'Congratulations,' Jordan said. 'What next?'

'I have to rinse. You're supposed to fill my mug with
warm water.'

Feeling hopelessly inadequate, Jordan observed the
nightly protocol. He steered the child to the toilet bowl.
'Time to...' he began, then stopped and rolled his eyes.
Go potty just wasn't part of his vocabulary. If resorting
to such inane language was prerequisite to being nomi-
nated father of the year, he hadn't a hope. 'Time to go,'
he improvised.

'You don't get to watch!' Patrick informed him,
outraged.

Jordan snatched at the chance to escape. 'Good,' he
said testily. 'It's not my idea of entertainment, either.
I'll wait for you in the bedroom.'

Patrick's voice wafted after him. 'You're supposed to
remind me to wash my hands.'

'Wash your hands, kid, and don't forget.'

Good God, if this was what parenting was all about,
it was small wonder his own mother's hair had turned
white before she was fifty! And story-time was still to
come. He wasn't sure he'd survive!

But after all, it wasn't so bad. The pop-up pictures
and the account of a boy and his dog who ran away to

become pirates entranced Patrick. 'You read better than Nonna,' he allowed when the story ended.

'Thanks. Some time I'll tell you the real live story of how I used to run away and hide in the mine when I was a kid.'

'You ran away?' Patrick's brown eyes, which had begun to droop sleepily, flew open, full of the closest thing to admiration Jordan had yet seen directed his way.

'You bet,' he said, catching himself just in time from swaggering, '"Old Man Mountain", we kids used to call it, because it was so stingy about giving up its gold, but I knew every hidey-hole it had to offer, and any time somebody really ticked me off, I'd high-tail it up there.'

'Promise you'll tell me about it, another night?'

'Promise.' Jordan turned down the lamp until only the small bulb in the base glowed, tucked the covers awkwardly around his boy's shoulders and began a furtive escape from the room. 'Goodnight, son.'

A muffled voice stopped him in his tracks. 'You forgot to kiss me goodnight.'

'Oh, yeah.' He turned back and bent low over the bed.

Patrick stared up at him, his eyes dark and still as pools. Unsure of the precise ritual a goodnight kiss entailed, Jordan bent lower and touched his lips to his son's cheek, then began a second catlike retreat.

Out of the gloom, a small arm snaked around his neck and held him fast. Warm, wet lips still faintly daubed with toothpaste connected with his jaw. 'Now you're supposed to hug,' Patrick murmured drowsily.

Jordan froze. For a long time, he'd carried a cold, hard weight lodged somewhere near his heart. Born of the regret and disillusionment over a marriage that had gone sour almost from the start and ended in utter tragedy, it had been such a constant companion that he'd learned to live with the ache—until that moment when the son he barely knew reached out for him. And then he experienced a tearing pain, accompanied by a swift, choking sensation in his throat, both directly associated with the small body clinging to him.

To his horror, tears stung his eyes, blurring the shadowed outlines of the room. Baffled by a weakness he'd never suspected in himself, Jordan buried his face in his son's neck. The child's skin was soft and smooth, his hair as fine as silk-spun thistledown. He smelled of soap and innocence.

At last, and with a profound sense of loss for the tender years he'd missed, Jordan raised his head. Patrick's lashes lay on his cheeks, feather-fine. His face in repose retained traces of babyhood, its contours not yet shaped by life, its expression cherubic. His breathing was quiet and even. Except for the small fist clutching the balding teddy bear, the child did not look so very different from the newborn infant that once, a long time ago, had filled his father's heart with so much hope and pride.

'Sleep well, son,' Jordan whispered hoarsely, backing stealthily toward the open door.

Halfway there, he sensed a shadow in the hall beyond. Had it turned out to be his mother, he might have felt annoyed at her intrusion on so private and special a moment. But when he realized it was Virginia, her hair gleaming palely in the gloom, her eyes, huge and solemn, fixed on him, he knew a flare of rage that went beyond anything rational.

'What the hell are you doing, lurking around up here?' he whispered savagely, steering her away from Patrick's room. 'In fact, what the hell are you doing in my house at all at this time of night?'

His fingers closed around her elbow with such crushing strength that she almost cried out. When squirming did not win her release, she said, 'You're hurting me, Jordan.'

'What?' He scowled, puzzled.

'You're hurting my elbow.'

'I am? Sorry!' Dismay gentled his fingers, although his gaze remained watchful. 'But that still doesn't answer my question. How long have you been standing there, snooping?'

Long enough, she could have told him, except that she knew he'd resent anyone having witnessed his brief lapse into humanity, or that moving exchange between him and his son. It had brought tears to her eyes, let alone his, but Jordan Caine wasn't the sort of man to view that as sympathetic commiseration. More likely it would intensify his prickly hostility.

So she lied to him. 'Not long at all. I came down the hall just as you were leaving Patrick's room.'

'Why? It's long past normal business hours and I don't remember inviting you to make a social call.'

The exasperation he so easily aroused nibbled at her compassion. 'After dinner tonight, I went through my notes and realized that we've never discussed what sort of décor you have in mind for your bedroom,' she explained with as much grace and patience as she could muster. 'So, I stopped by on the off-chance that you might be able to spare me another half-hour, and your mother sent me up here to find you. If you seriously expect to have the house completely finished by August the fifth, we need to settle all outstanding details now.'

He raked his hand through his hair, fairly bristling with irritation. 'Couldn't it have waited until tomorrow?'

'Not if I'm to believe what you told me earlier: that, after today, you expect to be too tied up with business to spare time for further consultations with me.'

'I'm already up to my neck in business and I've had enough distractions for one night.' He flung a glare at the closed door to Patrick's room. 'I can't believe how long it takes to settle a five-year-old boy.'

'It's time well spent, I'd say,' she observed rashly.

He switched his attention to her again, his handsomely drawn brows raised mockingly. 'Whatever makes you think I value your opinion on the matter, Virginia?'

Exasperation bloomed into outright annoyance. 'Only you could turn an innocent comment like that into a confrontation,' she retorted. 'Why do you find it necessary to work so hard projecting the image of a cold and distant parent? Are you afraid people might respect you less if they find out you're capable of tenderness? Or that, by acting like a normal, loving father, you're betraying some fatal flaw of weakness that will undermine your position in town?'

Even in the gloom, she saw the dark flush that stained his face and knew that she'd gone too far. There was nothing temperate in the way he grasped her arm a second time and literally marched her down the hall to the master suite that her parents had once occupied.

Shouldering open the door, he straight-armed her inside. Moonlight barred the floor and striped the walls. Except for a rolled-up carpet against one wall and a deep, cushioned window seat, the room was bare of furnishings. Not even the Austrian crystal chandelier that had once hung from the ceiling remained.

Maneuvering her close to the pale light from the window with rather more brawn than gallantry, he loomed over her, his eyes sparking fury. 'Exactly what qualifies you to arrive at such a conclusion, Virginia? Your own father's less-than-sterling attributes?'

'You know,' she said, quailing despite herself before the reined passion of his temper, 'that's not the first time you've made unflattering and unsubstantiated references to my father. Don't you think it's time you got whatever it is that's bothering you off your chest, since I assume it stems from something other than unadulterated envy for the life to which he was born and which you have only lately acquired?'

'If I thought that, by taking over the pathetic remains of your father's legacy to this town, I was in any danger of acquiring his attitudes, I believe I'd shoot myself. He was the most callous, self-centered man I've ever met. That he showed unlimited generosity to you and other

members of your family merely underlines his total indifference to the plight of those beyond it.'

'What makes you so sure you know how he treated
his family? How were you privy to what went on in this
house when I was a child?'

A grim smile curved Jordan's mouth. 'Don't you remember the afternoon when all little Virginia's friends
came to help her celebrate her ninth birthday? The party
favours and ice-cream? The uniformed maids scurrying
to do the bidding of the pint-sized guests? The clown,
and the photographer hired to record the momentous
occasion?'

The memories unwound, back to a time where the
images were pleasantly fuzzy and uncomplicated and
touched with the special magic of childhood. Back to a
day of sunlight…there it was, the moment captured and
brought into sharper focus by his reference. 'That was
the time we had the pony rides,' she marvelled.

His smile faded. 'That's right.'

'And you were there?'

'I was there,' he acknowledged sourly. 'I just wasn't
as memorable as the horse.'

Another image clicked in her mind. Strong arms
swinging her astride the saddle, firm hands guiding hers
on the reins. Blue eyes in a deeply tanned face. Unsmiling blue eyes. Angry blue eyes.

'You came with the pony,' she said.

'Right on, Miss Kent, ma'am. *Belonged* with the pony,
as far as your daddy was concerned. Me, my shovel, and
a plate of party left-overs, tethered behind the garage
out of sight until it was time to do my bit toward keeping
the nobility happy.'

'But that's no reason for you to hate me now! I was
just a little girl at the time.'

'Perhaps.' He loomed a little closer. 'But what about
the next time?'

She swallowed as memory fast-forwarded, a horrible
premonition taking hold. 'Next time?'

'Don't pretend you've forgotten that, too, Virginia. Why, you and your girlfriends spent the better part of the afternoon sniggering behind your hands and pretending not to notice that boys from the wrong side of the tracks were just as well endowed as those born on the hill.'

'I don't remember,' she said. But she did. With blinding clarity and scorching embarrassment. The buried dreams, the hopeless yearnings of adolescence when she'd still believed in Prince Charming and Happy Ever After, rose up to confront her: David still able to see, her parents content with each other—at least on the surface. And a sullen-mouthed youth who'd hauled her out when, squealing with shock, she'd accidentally slipped head-first into the pool while running carelessly around its tiled perimeter.

She hadn't needed rescuing, but he'd dived cleanly into the water and done it anyway. Not out of any sense of chivalry—indeed, his expression suggested he'd have preferred to watch her drown—but because that was what her father had paid him to do.

He'd grabbed her and hauled her to the surface. Without volition, her body had floated, weightless, against his and the next thing she knew, she was plastered against him with nothing but the thin, wet fabric of her swimsuit separating her fledgling breasts from the dusting of dark hair on his hard young chest.

The distressed sounds of her friends had faded to a distant, shimmering hum in the sunshine, transcended by a shooting physical response within her that both shocked and frightened her. She'd glanced down and felt the strange, heavy heat skim from the pit of her stomach to stain her neck and face scarlet. When she'd dared to look up again, he'd been staring at her, his eyelashes clumped with water, and a small, knowing sneer had crossed his face...

'Not remember?' Jordan taunted. 'Let me refresh your memory, then.' He ran a dispassionate finger down her throat and stopped it just short of the V-shaped collar of her blouse. 'Another birthday—your sixteenth, as I recall—just as hot and sunny as the first. Nature wouldn't have dared present anything less for one of the Kents. The pool that's been so sadly neglected in recent years sparkling like a gem...' his finger slipped lower, coming to rest at her cleavage '...and full of nubile girls, splashing in the cool, clear water, flaunting their budding femininity and pretentiously conscious of the lifeguard stationed near the diving board.'

'I don't know what you're talking about,' she lied in a cracked voice, a ribbon of heat searing a trail from his fingertip to her thighs.

Jordan slid his palm back up her throat and brought his thumb and middle finger to rest at the careening pulse points beneath her jaw. 'Sure you do,' he contradicted softly. 'In fact, you can probably describe the swimsuit you were wearing down to the last tiny detail. And from the way you kept on staring, you can certainly describe mine.'

Brief. Clinging. *Sculptured*.

The ribbon of heat intensified. 'No, I can't. I'm sorry to disappoint you, but I have no recollection of you at all.'

He looked momentarily crushed. 'Oh! Well, it was...let me think for a minute...' his elegant black brows knit together in concentration '...red—with black cuffs—and hung practically to my knees. I bought it new just for the occasion, because guys like me normally swam in the raw down at the lake and I didn't know baggy swim-trunks weren't in fashion. There I was in my cheap, outdated drawers, surrounded by laughing mermaids who made me feel like something out of a cartoon strip.'

'You're lying,' she said heatedly. 'You know damn well it was dark blue and fit like a second skin.'

His teeth gleamed in the moonlight. 'Well, golly-gee-whiz, Miss Virginia! I do believe you remember, after all.'

'It would be hard not to. You spent enough time strutting around and posing for us.'

'Not so, Highness. Squealing brats scarcely out of diapers didn't light my fire. I'd graduated to women by then and found them much more engrossing.'

She remembered *that*, too. It was later the same summer and there'd been a young people's social at the country club. To prolong the pleasure of the evening, she'd asked Jessup, the family chauffeur, to drive her and a girlfriend home through the park. Just as the car had turned into the pillared entrance, the headlamps had caught and silhouetted a man leaning against the ancient elm near the gates.

He'd turned his head and in the brief flare of light, Virginia had recognized the lifeguard with the unsmiling mouth and the disturbing blue eyes. And then she'd realized there was another body between his and the tree, and that the arm that had tugged him back to whatever he'd been doing belonged to a woman. It had been pale and slender, with something bright and shiny dangling from the wrist. And Virginia had felt all her pleasure seep away as a strange unhappy lurch tugged at her heart.

She had no idea what prompted her next remark but it had no sooner cooled on the air before she would have given her right hand to rescind it. '*I'm* a woman now,' she said, in a horrifyingly wanton whisper that trumpeted availability.

His hand froze at her throat.

'What I mean,' she babbled, 'is that you have no right to treat me so...disrespectfully, as if I'm some sort of mindless nitwit. In case you haven't noticed——'

'I've noticed,' he said hoarsely.

'Then why do you keep doing it? Why do you persist with this pointless hostility every time we're together?'

'Because it's safer than this,' he said, threading his fingers through her hair and pulling her against him.

His head blotted out the swath of moonlight so that she couldn't see his expression but he sighed like a man much put upon by circumstances not of his choosing, and his mouth settled on hers with studied indifference.

But his body! After a second or two of close acquaintance with hers, that lean and lovely male body about which she'd woven such daring teenage fantasies, stung her with redoubled awareness that she was not sixteen any longer. This was adult passion raking through her, born of adult appetites. It would take more than a sultry, insolent stare from a blue-eyed stranger to appease her hunger now.

As though he recognized that, and despite his best efforts to respond otherwise, Jordan's indifference melted and his sigh died. The hand that had reeled her in so abruptly slid caressingly to her head and secured her next to him with determined strength.

She was unprepared for the fiery sweetness of his kiss. Without warning, the backs of her knees sagged and she crumpled to the window seat. With ineffable grace, he sank down beside her. His other hand cupped her hip to bring her thigh across his, then fused a path up her ribs to the underslope of her breast.

If, at that moment, someone had screamed, 'Fire!', she could not have brought herself to care. What would it have mattered, when she was already aflame?

As though they'd practised on a hundred other men before him, her lips softened and parted. Accepted his tongue and knew exactly how to respond to its wooing. Her breasts strained against the fabric of her blouse, her nipples bloomed, crying out in the only way they knew how for him to release them, take them, love them. And she wanted to touch him back. Ached to find the courage to place her hand where it would please him most and just for a little while pretend that he and she had arrived at this moment through something other than an impromptu game of truth and dare.

The fingers still threaded through her hair tugged lightly, forcing back her head. His mouth drifted down her throat, bestowing kisses that whispered promises of pleasure beyond imagining.

'Ahh . . . !' she gasped, melting before a hunger more voracious than anything she'd have thought herself capable of. Covering his hand with hers, she guided it inside the deep neck of her blouse and pressed it to her bare flesh, uncaring that the movement upset her precarious balance and tipped her backward on the window-seat.

He gave a low growl of pleasure and shifted her effortlessly until she was pinned beneath him and he could look down on the pale, moon-kissed rise of her breast.

It was what she wanted, to be moulded against him, to revel in his strength, in the laboured beat of his heart. To feel the bruising conformation of arousal that he was helpless to conceal or deny.

His vulnerability gave her the courage to close her palms over the taut contours of his behind and hold him fast against her. There was such a flailing of her heart behind her ribs and such a yearning in her body that she wished she could ignore her conscience and simply wrap her legs around him and let nature take its course. But when he moved away from her in order to facilitate just such a happening, the night air brushed her skin coolly and restored her to her senses.

She could not pretend ignorance. He had a right to know before it was too late.

She shoved aside his hand and clamped her knees together, realizing that she was inviting his scorn and deserved any ugly name he might choose to call her. 'Wait, Jordan,' she begged. 'There's something I have to tell you.'

He hovered above her, moonlight silvering his hair. 'Don't tell me you're not on the Pill,' he said hoarsely.

'Worse,' she said, on a pathetic little quaver. 'I'm still a virgin.'

CHAPTER SIX

At that, Jordan lifted his head, the hissed intake of his breath a jarring dissonance in the otherwise quiet room. He jerked himself upright and shot his immaculate shirt cuffs into place. 'Well, hell!' he said softly. 'I didn't know chastity had such a long shelf-life.'

Virginia refused to allow him to goad her into trading insults and she certainly was not about to offer any explanations. 'In my case it does . . . and I thought you had a right to know . . . before . . .'

'Before what?'

Had there ever been a moon quite so unkind, to expose her sprawling disarray at the same time that it showered him with noble hauteur? Groping to cover her thighs, she sat up and struggled to define an answer that would reinstate her dignity without belittling the sincerity of her emotions.

There wasn't one. How could she have thought there would be? She lowered her head and watched as her fingers formed distracted pleats with the fabric of her skirt. 'Before things went any further.'

'Indeed,' he said, with biting irony. 'Heaven forfend that the virgin princess should be deflowered by anything less than a stud of equally royal blood.'

'That's not what I was trying to say,' she replied miserably. 'I wanted . . .'

'What did you want, Highness? To show the stable boy what he was missing?'

I wanted you, she longed to tell him. Don't ask me how or why because all I can tell you is that you awoke something in me thirteen years ago that's been waiting for you ever since. But how could she expect him to believe that, when she hadn't fully realized it herself until

78

a few minutes ago? And to voice the other truth—that his touch ignited such a raging need in her that she couldn't be held accountable for her actions—required more courage than she possessed. 'I didn't want there to be any misunderstandings between us later,' she improvised.

'Very wise of you, I'm sure,' he replied scathingly. '*Noblesse oblige* isn't something they taught us in the school I attended and I don't think I'd be very good at it.'

'I didn't mean that I'd have expected you to marry me if we'd made love.'

'That's not what we would have done,' he assured her flatly. 'At best, we'd have had sex, and even someone of your unsullied virtue should know the difference— always assuming, of course, that you're telling the truth to begin with.'

She stared at him, astounded. 'Why on earth would I lie?'

'The belated realization that, even in their indiscretions, Kents don't go slumming comes to mind.'

'Such a thought never entered my head!'

'Of those that do, few appear to remain in residence longer than a minute,' he drawled obscurely, flicking some minute speck from his sleeve. 'I want gray or blue.'

'Grey or blue?' she echoed, mystified.

'The colour scheme for my room, though I suppose you can be forgiven for having forgotten it was the reason you supposedly sought me out to begin with. You did switch to propositioning me rather soon after you got here, after all.'

She felt her face flame in the pale moonlight. 'I didn't!'

'Yes, you did, Highness,' he said implacably. 'And your belated and not very convincingly naïve performance is beginning to bore me, so, to get back to the alleged purpose of your visit, steer clear of brown, stick mainly to blues or grays, and keep it simple. Contrary to what you seem to think, this is my bedroom, not a stud farm.'

'You really are unbelievably vulgar,' she advised him.

His grin flashed in the gloom. 'That's right. And what a good thing you remembered in time, or how would you have lived with yourself tomorrow?'

Virginia didn't know. It was difficult enough living with what had transpired, and it took every scrap of courage for her to show up for work as usual the next morning. But Jordan was long gone to the mine before she arrived at the mansion, and remained away until after she'd left, a practice he continued for the next few days. If the peace that reigned as a result left her feeling oddly unhappy, she chose to believe it had everything to do with seeing the last remaining traces of her childhood home erased by the ultra-chic décor ordered by the new owner, and nothing at all to do with missing her abrasive client.

Not surprisingly, Jordan also declined to accept David's impetuous dinner invitation for the following Friday—though somewhat less graciously than his mother relayed his regrets, Virginia was sure.

'I am sorry, *cara*,' Maria said. 'My son simply cannot spare the time.'

Upon hearing this, Virginia once again told herself that what felt like sagging disappointment was really profound relief. Sitting across the table from Jordan and making polite small talk, all the while knowing she'd thrown herself unashamedly at him, would have been a social nightmare. 'Never mind,' she told Maria with false cheer. 'Come by yourself instead.'

'You are kind, and I wish I could.' Maria shrugged unhappily. 'But I think I must say no. When Joey comes home, he is tired and hungry and there are only a few more days that I can enjoy making meals for him in this beautiful kitchen.'

'For heaven's sake, Maria, why?'

'He has hired a cook and she is to start work next week. Also a housekeeper whose husband is to be the gardener as well as my driver whenever I want to go out. They will live in the little house near the front gates.' Her voice wobbled dismayingly. 'I am to become a lady of leisure because my son does not think it is proper that his mother should soil her hands with work, but this old lady does not know how to be idle.'

'Have you tried to explain to him how you feel?' Virginia asked softly.

'Of course. And he listens—but he does not hear.' Maria's voice broke completely then and tears swam in her eyes. 'I feel lonely, Virginia, even though, for the first time in many years, I am with my family. Nobody needs me any more.'

Jordan would have considered it an unpardonable liberty, no doubt, but Virginia couldn't stand by and not reach out to comfort the old lady. 'That's not true!' she exclaimed, hugging her. 'Patrick would be lost without you and so would I. You've become a friend, someone I feel I can turn to. There hasn't been anyone like you in my life since my mother died.'

'Ai! Now you make me cry in earnest!'

'I don't mean to. I just don't like to see you so unhappy.'

'You are a good girl,' Maria sniffed, reaching for her dishtowel to mop at the tears dribbling down her face, 'and my son is a fool not to snap you up before——'

Virginia knew what was coming. She'd seen the speculative gleam in his mother's eyes as they flitted from Jordan to his interior fashion consultant. If Maria had her way, Virginia would be decorating a lot more than his house; she'd be reshaping his entire life. 'I have an idea,' she interrupted hurriedly. 'If you won't come for dinner, come for tea one afternoon instead, and bring Patrick with you. One of our best dogs just had a litter and the pups are adorable. I'm sure he'd love to see them.'

'That I could do!' A spark of pleasure chased away Maria's distress. 'Which day shall it be?'

'Let's make it a week from Saturday, around four. By then, the puppies will be old enough to be handled, and things around here ought to have progressed far enough that I can steal a few hours away from the job without having Jordan out for my blood.'

After an uncertain start, the day in question turned into a lovely afternoon. The massed bank of hydrangeas lining the west side of the garden were at the peak of their purple-blue perfection and the pergola covering the path to the kennels was scarcely visible under a cloak of scarlet rambler roses.

'Much too nice to be indoors,' Virginia decided, and helped Susan serve tea under the cherry tree that overlooked the lake at the bottom of the lawn.

Maria was enchanted. 'But this is so old-fashioned and charming!' she exclaimed, her gaze roaming from the profusion of flowers bordering the grass to the Battenburg lace cloth and delicate Spode china gracing the table. 'From the way my Joey spoke, I thought your home would be——' She stopped abruptly, dismay at her near indiscretion clouding her eyes. 'Well, it does not matter what I thought. Signor David, I am happy to see you again.'

'I'm glad Virginia persuaded you to visit.' David waited until he heard her chair creak under her weight before taking a seat next to her. 'Did you bring Patrick with you?'

'Yes. He is trying to hide behind my skirts.' Maria laughed, her composure restored. 'I think he is still a little afraid of your dog. He is such a big creature.'

David smiled. 'Would you believe, Patrick, that Lucas was once so small I could hold him on the palm of my hand?'

Eyes like saucers, Patrick peeped from David's outstretched palm to Lucas and shook his head. With the amazing telepathy he so often displayed, David sensed the child's disbelief. 'What if I told you we have puppies so small you could hold them in *your* hands? Would you like to see them?'

'Will they bite me?'

'No. They don't have any teeth yet. In fact, they only just opened their eyes.'

'Where are they?'

'In the kennel around the other side of the house.' David stood up. 'Come with me and I'll show you.'

Patrick inched out from behind his grandmother. 'But you can't see, so how will you know the way?'

'Because I've walked over there so often I could do it in my sleep—and because Lucas will make sure I don't take a wrong turn.' David caressed the dog's ears, then grasped the leather harness in his left hand. 'The puppies usually wake from their nap about now. I think they might like a little company.'

The temptation was too much for a small boy to resist. Giving Lucas a wide berth, Patrick scuttled to David's other side and clutched his right hand. 'Are you *sure* they don't have any teeth?' he enquired earnestly.

'He is so timid,' Maria sighed, once the trio had disappeared along the rose-shaded path. 'It makes Joey very impatient.'

'I know.' Virginia poured tea and offered a cup to her guest. 'I think it must be hard for a man like him to understand another person's fears. I don't believe he's ever been afraid of anything.'

Maria helped herself to freshly baked scones, homemade strawberry jam and farm cream before replying, 'You are wrong, Virginia. Although my Joey is brave in every other way, there is one thing that frightens him terribly, and that is to dare to love his son.'

Virginia couldn't hide her shock. 'That's not true! Why, I've seen for myself——'

'He is afraid, *cara*. He has buried one child and it almost killed him. He will not allow himself to care too much for the one that is left, and that makes me afraid for both of them.'

'I had no idea there'd been another child,' Virginia whispered, shaken. 'What happened?'

'There was a car crash.'

'Was . . . was Jordan driving?'

'No.' Maria shook her head sadly. 'It was his wife. She was dispirited after her baby's birth in the way that some women are, and she drove too fast. Their little girl was only two months old at the time.'

'I do not have a wife,' Jordan had told her, the day she'd suggested consulting with the lady of the house on the kitchen design, and now Virginia knew why. Grief had wrought too much damage for the marriage to survive. 'The divorce must have been very painful for both of them.'

'There was no divorce, Virginia. Penelope, his wife, she was killed, too, poor thing.'

Virginia closed her eyes in horror. 'Oh, Maria! How dreadful for all of you!'

'Yes. And that poor girl's parents, how they suffered, too. And how they blamed Joey, even though nothing he could have said or done would have stopped Penelope once she'd made up her mind. And he tried to atone by giving them his son. "To help me out," is how he explained it to me at the time, because his work took him away so much and he was at his wits' end trying to look after such a little boy, but I believe it was also because he felt he did not deserve a child. And Penelope's parents, they said as much to his face.'

'Why were they so cruel?'

'Because they could not face their own guilt,' Maria said, sorrow and wisdom shadowing her lovely eyes. 'They had raised a daughter who would not grow up, one who always had to have things her own way. They lavished her with everything they had to give—their love, their wealth, their intercession when things did not turn out as she wished. "My rich, spoiled beauty," Joey used to call her, when first they were married. But at the end . . .' She shook her head. 'At the end, the beauty was lost in the ugliness between them. Joey thinks I did not see, but a mother always knows when things are not going well for her child.'

Wishing she could find something to say that didn't sound hopelessly trite, Virginia reached across and covered Maria's hand with her own. 'I'm so sorry.'

Maria sighed. 'My Joey was not without blame. So ambitious he was—always wanting to reach higher, be better—that it is true he spent more time at work than with his family. But he did not deserve to pay such a heavy price.'

Perhaps it was a good thing that Patrick's high, excited voice rang in the air just then. It necessitated a change of subject that occurred not a moment too soon. As David and the boy made their way back under the pergola, Susan came through the French doors leading from the living-room with Jordan at her side.

Maria slopped tea in her saucer and exchanged guilty glances with Virginia, who felt herself blushing to the roots of her hair. 'I thought you were supposed to be busy at the mine,' she blurted out, as he strolled across the lawn to join them. 'What are you doing here?'

Maria mopped at the mess she'd made and tried to appear undisturbed by her son's probing stare. 'I did not expect you, *mio figlio*,' she murmured. 'There is not more trouble, I hope?'

He leaned against the trunk of the cherry tree, the lake at his back outrivalled by the intense blue of his eyes. 'I hope not, too, Momma,' he said in a meaningful voice.

He's suspicious, Virginia realized, casting about in her mind for a way to distract him. 'Would you like some tea, Jordan? I'd be glad to make a fresh pot and bring a cup for you.'

By then, David was within earshot and with the infallible instinct he'd developed since he lost his sight, picked up on the tension shimmering in the air. 'Who needs tea in this heat?' he enquired cheerfully. 'I'm going to have a beer instead. Will you join me, Mr Caine?'

'No,' Maria said, still thoroughly discombobulated by her son's unexpected appearance. 'We must go home now.'

'Yes, thank you,' Jordan overruled, a malicious gleam in his eye. 'I'm not in such a hurry, Momma, that you can't finish your tea—or your conversation. What was it the two of you had your heads together about?'

Virginia stared him straight in the eye and lied without a qualm. 'The Miners' Ball.'

'What about it?' he pursued, staring right back.

'Clothes,' she said, digging herself in deeper. 'You know, what to wear, and all that.'

'That's usually what clothes are all about,' he conceded, pulling out the chair next to hers and settling in for the duration. 'So, what did you decide?'

'That your mother and I will go to Halford some time very soon and shop for a suitable ballgown for her.'

'I see.' The sun slipped low enough on the horizon to penetrate the shade under the tree. Jordan reached into the breast pocket of his shirt for a pair of dark sunglasses, propped them on his nose, then linked his fingers loosely over his flat midriff. 'Does the prospect of shopping for someone else always leave you so charmingly rosy, Virginia?'

Her blush, which had started to fade, promptly burgeoned anew. 'Actually, we were hoping to surprise you.'

An enigmatic little smile hovered briefly on Jordan's mouth. 'And instead, I surprised you.'

Radar fully operational, David once again tried to come to Virginia's rescue. 'I think it's a bit late in the day for beer,' he decided. 'What do you say we all go up to the house and enjoy a before-dinner aperitif, instead?'

'I don't have time,' Jordan said, civilly enough.

'Well, I'd appreciate it if you'd make the time,' David replied. 'Patrick and I have a proposition we'd like to put to you—and a cocktail won't take any longer to down than the beer you just agreed to.'

Jordan switched his attention to Patrick, who was fairly dancing with excitement. 'All right. I guess I can spare half an hour.'

'The rest of you go ahead and leave me to bring up the tea things,' Virginia suggested, anxious to be rid of Jordan before he mired her in more awkward dialogue. 'It won't take more than a few minutes.'

Either he wasn't taken in for a minute or he possessed greater chivalry than he'd hitherto shown. Of the two, the former seemed more probable. 'It'll take even less if I give you a hand,' he said, his voice and smile as blandly expressionless as his gaze behind the opaque sun glasses. 'Go ahead with Mr Kent, Momma, and take Patrick with you. His hands look as if they could use a good wash.'

The second the trio disappeared inside the house, Jordan's benevolent air fell away. 'All right,' he snapped, whipping off the glasses and subjecting her to a gimlet-eyed stare, 'out with it. What was it you and my mother were discussing that's got the pair of you hopping around like fleas on a dog—and never mind the old "we're going shopping for a dress" routine. Clothes have never been a subject to get Momma all frayed around the edges.'

'Precisely,' Virginia said, rallying before his smug certainty that, now that he had her cornered, he'd have no trouble wresting the truth from her. 'She's finding the idea of having to get dressed to the nines quite an ordeal. Why did *you* show up here? In the hopes that you'd catch us up to no good?'

'No, that was an unexpected bonus,' he said, clearly unmoved by her attempt to bamboozle him. 'I'd expected only to collect my mother and son and drive them home.'

'Why would you put yourself to the bother when you've hired someone else for that very purpose?'

'Because I had to send Thurston into town to pick up a set of plans that I'll need at the mine tomorrow.' His hand closed implacably over hers. 'You've stacked and restacked those cups four times, Virginia. What's making you so nervous?'

She wished she could be at least partially honest and tell him that the knowledge of what he'd suffered allowed her new insight into what made him the man he was today; that her heart ached for him and she wanted nothing more than to hold his face between her hands and stroke away the sorrow that she knew must haunt him.

But he wouldn't thank her for her sympathy and, aside from a reluctance to betray Maria's confidence, Virginia found herself brought up squarely against a truth she'd been fighting to avoid for some time. Her feelings for Jordan, which had, practically from the beginning, created within her utter turmoil of one kind or another, had come the three-quarters full circle from outright dislike to...

What?

She shied away from the answer that immediately sprang to mind. Not love! There was no reason to love a man whose caustic tongue and scorn were too often directed at her. A more likely explanation was pity— except that why pity should make her want to wrap her arms around him and beg, Don't shut me out because of Penelope. Give me the chance to show you I'm not like her, didn't add up at all.

'You're enough to make anyone nervous,' she retorted, closing her mind to such disturbing insights. 'I wish you'd stop giving me the third degree as if I'm some sort of criminal.'

'If your conscience is as clear as you claim, you've got nothing to worry about. Tell me, are you planning to buy a dress for yourself when you take my mother shopping?'

'No. Why should I?'

'Because she invited you to attend the Miners' Ball.'

'An invitation I intend to decline, since I'm sure you begrudge its having been extended.' She picked up the tea-tray and thrust it into his hands, adding pointedly, 'Here, make yourself useful and carry this up to the house. I'm being a very poor hostess, ignoring my *invited* guests to hang around here trying to ease your suspicious mind. If you've got any more questions, ask them when we're inside.'

Since he'd never before shown himself inclined to be reasonable if he could possibly find cause to behave otherwise, his ready acquiescence to her demand left her full of suspicion. Sure enough, he was no sooner seated next to his mother on the couch in the living-room before his devious mind went to work ferreting out the truth.

Leaning forward so that his shoulders blocked her view and prevented Maria from making eye contact with anyone else, he injected a conviviality into his words that struck a ludicrous note to Virginia's ear. 'So, Momma,' he announced, 'I gather you've persuaded Virginia to accept our invitation to the Miners' Ball?'

Maria swallowed the bait hook, line and sinker. 'Yes,' she said, any surprise she felt at the news outweighed by her obvious pleasure.

'So you'll be shopping for not one gown but two.'

'Yes,' his trusting mother said again.

He aimed a patently phony smile Virginia's way. 'If you'll pour me a drink, I'll propose a toast to celebrate.'

She fixed him in a stony glare. 'What would you like?'

'Surprise me—again,' he suggested snidely.

'I'd love to,' she said with equal malice, 'but we're fresh out of henbane.'

Jordan's lips twitched but, before he could respond, David stepped in to defuse what he'd accurately detected to be another potentially volatile situation. 'Mix up a

pitcher of vodka-tonics, Virginia. They're the only civi-
lised choice in temperatures like this,' he said then, before
Jordan could get another word in edgewise, swung
toward him and went on, 'About that proposition Patrick
and I wanted to make——'

'Speaking of whom,' Jordan cut in, apparently no-
ticing for the first time that Patrick was not in the room,
'where is my son?'

'In the kitchen with Susan. I believe she lured him
there with mention of chocolate chip cookies. She's his
latest friend, but he did make another, earlier this
afternoon and, if you're agreeable, I think it would be
good for both parties to spend some time together. I
have a dog, you see——'

'Besides this one, you mean?' Jordan enquired, condescending to scratch Lucas behind the ears.

'Several, as a matter of fact,' David said. 'I breed and
train German shepherds which, as you probably know,
are classed as working dogs. Four from my kennels have
graduated as seeing-eye dogs, and another is a valued
member of a search and rescue team. But the animal I'm
talking about isn't quite ready for the sort of intensive
training involved in these types of work. He's too young,
too playful. And I don't want to take a chance on spoiling
his excellent temperament by pushing him too hard too
soon.'

'I hope you aren't asking us to take him,' Jordan said.
'I've got nothing against having a pet around the place,
but now isn't a good time for one. You've seen—er—
you *understand* the house is little better than a con-
struction site.'

David's easy laugh dispelled any awkwardness
Jordan's verbal slip might have aroused. 'Of course, and
I'm not suggesting you take Tramp home with you. Not
only are we too fond of him to farm him out, it would
also be much too hard on Patrick when the time came
to return him to us. Instead, I'd like it if your son could
come down here three or four days a week and spend

time with the dog. Play games with him that will help prepare him for the more serious training he'll face over the winter, teach him basic commands, and that sort of thing.'

'I think it would be a great idea,' Jordan allowed, only to add bluntly, 'if it weren't for the fact that Patrick strikes me as scared stiff of his own shadow, let alone a dog the size of a small horse.'

'Well, if playing with Tramp helped him overcome that, it would be a mutually beneficial experience, wouldn't you say?'

'If it works, yes. But what makes you sure it will?'

'I introduced them this afternoon, after we'd visited Tora and her new litter. I wish you'd been there. I think you'd have been pleasantly surprised at the interaction between boy and dog.'

'In that case...' Jordan raised enquiring brows at Maria '...what do you say we give it a trial, Momma, if it doesn't interfere with your plans too much? Because it would mean having Patrick dropped off and picked up. I don't want him walking down here by himself and the hill's too steep for you to take on foot.'

'Apart from which, we'd love to have you come with him, Maria,' Virginia hastened to point out, 'provided you have nothing else planned.'

Maria's smile spoke louder than the words that accompanied it. 'I think it will be good for both of us to get out once in a while.'

At that moment, Susan appeared with a tray of hors-d'oeuvres and shortly after became engaged in a recipe exchange with Maria. Patrick, who'd come in with Susan, climbed on his grandmother's lap, his normally pale cheeks rosy.

For the moment content to relax and sip his drink, Jordan sprawled elegantly on the couch and took inventory of his surroundings. His gaze flitted idly from the crystal bowl of sweet peas on the mantelpiece, past the gilt-framed oil portrait of Virginia as an eighteen-year-old débutante, to the priceless Flemish wine cabinet that had been a wedding gift to her and David's maternal great-grandmother.

David, who was sitting on the bench in front of the grand piano, swung around to face the keys and began to play softly.

A stranger looking in could have been forgiven for thinking they were all the best of friends. Virginia might almost have been lulled into believing it herself—until Jordan slid across to the chair next to hers and spoke softly in her ear. 'Want to come clean now, and tell me what you and my mother were really talking about outside?'

She sighed, realizing how vain had been her hope that he'd let the matter drop. 'No,' she said shortly.

'I hope this afternoon's little charade taught you that deceit seldom pays off; that, sooner or later, people always trip over their own lies.'

'You're speaking from humiliating personal experience, I'm sure,' she countered, risking a glance in his direction.

His gaze locked on hers and refused to let go. 'I lied only to prove that you weren't being truthful in the first place.'

'I don't care what your reasons were. My conscience would never have allowed me to embroil *my* mother in dishonesty, no matter what the reason.'

He leaned closer and dropped his voice another notch, from baritone to intimate bass. 'Probably because you learned at your father's knee to have no conscience at all.'

Virginia turned fully toward him and lowered her eyelids in a slow blink intended to convey utter contempt. 'In polite society, guests do not insult their hostess, no matter how great the provocation.'

'You are quite right and I apologize. What do you say we take off the gloves and stop sparring?'

He was not a man to accept censure kindly and such unruffled acceptance of her snub had her breaking out in a shiver of apprehension. 'Why?'

Of course, he noticed her reaction, and a seraph from hell could not have smiled with more malicious delight. 'Because we're neighbors and cannot avoid intercourse,' he purred, wreaking the ultimate havoc on her poise.

'*Intercourse*?' she squeaked, then clapped an appalled hand to her mouth, grateful that David's piano-playing made it unlikely that anyone else in the room had heard her.

'Of the purely social kind, of course,' Jordan Caine assured her blandly.

Heat swept from the soles of her feet to her face, trailing fire in its wake. 'Of course,' she echoed weakly.

He swept a casual hand before him. 'You have a lovely home, my dear.'

'Thank you,' she said, amazed that her voice emerged at all over the racing pandemonium of her heart.

'I confess I'm pleasantly surprised.'

'Are you?'

'Yes. I had not expected anything quite so…gracious.'

'What you mean is that you thought—or more likely hoped—that we were living in abject poverty.'

'No, Virginia,' he said reproachfully. 'I would not wish that on anyone, not even Andrew Kent's children. I know what a corrosive effect poverty has on the quality of life and I suppose I must afford your father credit for making sure it didn't encroach on yours or your brother's.'

Of all the things he'd said or done to strip her of her composure, this provoked her the most. 'My father has nothing at all to do with the way we live,' she said fiercely. 'He has never set foot in this house. For all he knows or cares, we could be living on welfare.'

'Oh, dear,' Jordan murmured ironically. 'I might almost be persuaded to think we agree on something at last and that neither of us holds Andrew Kent in high regard—except that while mine is fuelled by deep and abiding resentment, yours, I suspect, is founded on mere pique. What did he do, Virginia? Cut off your allowance?'

Virginia thought of the wounds her father had inflicted on the people she loved best in the world, and all the rage that for years she'd subdued unexpectedly boiled up and spilled over. And because Andrew Kent wasn't there to receive it, Jordan Caine fell unhappy victim to the outpouring. 'No,' she whispered, her voice and hands shaking with a fury that set the ice-cubes in her glass to rattling, and her face suddenly streaming with tears. 'Among other things, he killed my mother.'

CHAPTER SEVEN

SHE didn't have time to be embarrassed at the spectacle she might be making of herself because Jordan immediately reached over, took the glass of vodka and tonic from her and placed it on the coffee-table.

'Show me,' he said, using the width and height of his body to shield her from Maria and Susan's curious gaze as he hustled her across the room toward the garden doors. 'I don't believe tropical flowers can thrive this far north, even in a summer as hot as ours.'

And then they were outside with the cool air of dusk brushing her face and Jordan, his arm at her waist, leading her firmly down a flight of shallow, uneven steps to a little stone bench beside the lily pond, on the far side of a stand of tall bamboo.

Not that Virginia could see any of it. She was too blinded by the tears that, having once begun, showed no inclination to stop. Soaking the handkerchief with which he attempted to mop them up, they continued to pour soundlessly and endlessly down her cheeks. Finally, Jordan stopped trying and simply held her with her face buried against his chest until the storm passed and coherence returned.

'I'm sorry,' she eventually managed. 'I don't know what precipitated such an emotional display.'

'I do,' he said, stroking dripping strands of hair away from her face and tucking them behind her ears. 'I behaved like a boor, as I usually do whenever I'm around you—except that, this time, I did a better than normal job of trampling all over your feelings.'

She felt his chest rise and fall in a sigh. 'Damn,' he muttered. 'If hurting you is the only way to vent my hatred for your father, maybe it *is* time to let go of the past. It's years too late for me to be able to change it, after all, and from what you just told me, you're as much his victim as anyone else.'

'Not me so much as David—and my mother, of course.'

'Want to tell me about it, if I promise not to interrupt with any smart-ass comments?'

She wadded his handkerchief into a ball and shrugged uncertainly. 'I don't know how. I've never talked to anyone else, except David.'

'It might help if you did,' Jordan said, pulling her down beside him on the bench. 'There's no one here but me and an early moon, and neither of us is going to breathe a word of what you say to anyone else.'

'Thank you, but you wouldn't find it very interesting. I doubt you'd even understand.' Weepy exhaustion rendered her voice frail as a dying leaf falling from the tree and left her leaning weakly against him.

She hated the way she was behaving, like some gray and pathetic waif, but she couldn't help herself. She was tired of having to watch her every word with him, and frankly horrified by the ease with which he inveigled her forgiveness despite his past performance as her unbridled antagonist. To allow him access to the skeletons in her family closet would do nothing but supply him with ammunition for the next time he wanted to torment her. It was easier, safer, to back away despite the bizarre weakness in her that ached to respond to this other, more humane side of him.

But Jordan had never before allowed her to take the easy route and he wasn't about to start now. 'I want to understand,' he said earnestly, his blue gaze boring deep into her soul. 'I *need* to understand, Virginia.'

'Why?' she asked, striving for indifference.

'Because Andrew Kent killed my father, too.'

If he'd wanted to shock her out of her apathy, he chose the right way to go about it. Dismayed, she swung back to face him. 'What did you say?'

'He killed my father, too. And although I thought there was a certain poetic justice in making you pay for his crime, it appears I might have been wrong.'

The shaking took hold of her again, spreading clammy dismay over her skin like a shroud. 'Killed your father how ... ?'

Jordan shook his head. 'No,' he said, running a compassionate hand up her arm. 'There's time for all that later. Tell me about you, first.'

His touch warmed her, fortifying her against the memories. She began slowly, her words slow and inadequate, her sentences disjointed. 'I don't know when it began. I really loved my father when I was little. I didn't want to see—he was never unkind to me, you know, not the way you think he was to you. He probably didn't even realize that he treated you like a servant—well, maybe he did because, in a way, that's what you were— no, what I mean is that he paid you to come and work for him, so in his eyes that's what you were——'

Jordan cupped her face in both his hands and held it firmly. 'Virginia, take a deep breath and start over. This isn't about me, it's about you and your family, so never mind trying to spare my feelings. When did things change for *you* with your father? Seeing him through more adult eyes? Or was there some specific occasion that stripped you of your illusions?'

'It was my brother's accident,' she said. 'Once we knew that David would never see again, my father cast him off as though he were a piece of faulty equipment. ''A fat lot of good you've turned out to be,'' he said, when they finally released David from the rehab centre where he'd spent two months beginning to cope with his handicap. And after that, Father barely acknowledged him. It was as though having a blind son reflected badly on him in some way, made him less of a success.

'One night I came in late from a high school concert and heard my parents arguing, shouting at each other in a way they'd never done before. I crept up the stairs, afraid of what had provoked it, and saw them facing each other across the bedroom. ''I think you'd rather he'd died,'' my mother accused, and I knew at once that they were talking about David because my father yelled back, ''You're damned right, I would! He's an albatross around the neck of everyone in this family and I'll never forgive him for saddling us with the pity of every god-damned blue-collar worker in this town.'''

'That must have been very painful for you,' Jordan said, his gaze roaming her face.

'For me?' A parody of laughter croaked in Virginia's throat and she turned away from the pity she saw in his eyes. 'How do you think David felt?'

'You didn't tell him, surely?'

'Of course not! But he heard anyway. The shouting had woken him and when I turned to escape the hatred and the anger I'd witnessed, I found him standing at the end of the hall outside his bedroom door. I remember running to him and hugging him and crying for him. And he ended up comforting me, even though I was older by four years. ''It's OK,'' he said. ''Dad's a perfectionist, we both know that. He doesn't know how to cope with someone who'll never live up to his high expectations.'''

'Was he right?'

'Probably. It wasn't too long after that that my mother's health began to fail, which was all it took to spell the end of her marriage.'

'Are you telling me that your father walked out because his wife was ill?' Jordan asked in disgust. 'Good God, whatever happened to ''in sickness and in health''?'

Virginia shook her head. 'He didn't walk out exactly. He got involved in some business scheme in Arizona and what began as flying visits to check on his investment gradually turned into trips that lasted weeks. Each time he was home, the fighting grew worse. One time, he came back to find Mother had moved into the suite of rooms that Maria now uses, and after that they barely spoke to one another.'

'How did he treat you during all this?'

'At first, just as he always had, but things were never the same for me after that time he'd said those awful things about David, and eventually he noticed. He tried to talk to me about it.' Virginia shuddered. 'He said that the most important lesson in life was recognizing when to cut your losses. "If a car starts breaking down all the time and can't perform as it was meant to," he told me, "the smart man trades it in for something he can rely on. It's the same with everything else, Virginia. Life's too short for a person to burden himself with failures."'

Jordan snorted contemptuously. 'Did no one ever teach him the difference between things and people? Did he think David chose to be blinded in an accident, or that your mother went out of her way to get sick?'

'I asked him pretty much the same questions,' Virginia replied.

'And how did he answer?'

She squeezed her eyes shut against the picture crowding her mind. Of her, tearful and pleading; of her father, cold and immovable. Of his voice lacerating her with scorn when he said, 'You're on *their* side, aren't you? My God, first a liability of a son, and now a fool for a daughter.'

'"Haven't you forgotten my mother?" I asked him, hoping to shame him with the sarcasm I was sure he couldn't miss, but he just...*laughed*, and said he wished he could. "Why do you think I spend so much time away from home?" he jeered...'

She heard the tremor in her voice and pressed a hand to her mouth as it all came flooding back, as stark as if it had happened just yesterday.

Jordan slid his palms under her elbows and tried to pull her into his arms. 'Never mind the rest. It doesn't matter any more.'

'It does to me,' she said, resisting him. 'I've tried so hard to justify his actions. Was it the pressure of running the mine that made him so unfeeling, or was it simply his way of coping with disaster? Was he really grieving on the inside and just too proud to let it show?'

'No,' Jordan said flatly. 'He was a monstrous, cold-blooded son-of-a-bitch.'

There was a time not too long ago when Virginia would have found such language supremely offensive. Now, it merely fit the description of a man whose insensitivity to others had never been more fully apparent than in the weeks following his wife's death.

'You're quite right,' she said, trying to remain calm and dispassionate. It had been ten years, after all. But the pain of remembering was a knife-blade in her heart and her voice faltered again. 'My mother wasn't cold in her grave before...'

'Before what, darling?' Jordan's voice rode her anguish in low, soothing tones.

'Before he brought his mistress to the house and paraded her before his children.'

Jordan reared back as if he'd been bitten by a cobra and, even though it was dusk by then, she saw the pupils of his eyes widen until the blue irises were reduced to narrow, brilliant rings of colour. 'Oh, no!' he breathed in a shocked whisper. 'Surely not!'

'I'm afraid so.'

He shook his head in mute disbelief and for a minute or two there was nothing but the splash of the little stone fountain at the far end of the lily pond to disturb the quiet of the evening. Next to the bench, a light enclosed in a miniature stone pagoda glimmered softly over the deep green of the surrounding shrubbery but the presence of the house beyond intruded not at all. She and Jordan might have been miles removed from civilization.

Tentatively, she touched his shoulder. 'Your turn,' she said. 'Unless talking is too painful?'

'No more than it was for you,' he told her huskily. 'How you must hate him—more even than I do.'

'No,' Virginia said. 'I refuse to accord him that honour. He isn't worth the energy.'

Jordan had swung away and was sitting with his elbows on his knees, staring at the ground between his feet, but at her words, her touch, he turned and looked at her long and thoughtfully. 'I had no idea,' he said, a trifle unsteadily, 'of the wisdom behind that lovely, calm exterior of yours. No understanding...' He shifted toward her and almost groped for her, as though he wasn't sure she was real and feared she might disappear with the fading daylight. 'Of the pain you hide so well.'

'Not always well,' she said. 'Just differently from you.'

'Yes,' he said. 'I feed on my anger, and in turn it consumes me. It would be better for everyone if I could let it go. Perhaps talking to you will allow me to do that.'

Yet he sounded uncertain. He scowled at the lily-pads floating serenely on the dark surface of the water, and was silent for so long that Virginia thought perhaps he'd changed his mind. But then she noticed the way he'd laced his fingers tightly together until the skin over his knuckles gleamed a shade more palely against the tan of his hands, and she realized it was as hard for him to share his private agony as it had been for her.

Composing herself to patience, she sat quietly and waited. At last his voice drifted over to her, half disembodied in the gloom. 'Once upon a time,' he began, 'forty years ago to be exact, Patrick Sean Caine, a young Irishman newly arrived in Canada, fell in love with Maria Sophia Carbone, the daughter of an Italian immigrant. They were married with the blessings of her family and moved to the west because they believed it was the land of opportunity. They settled in Opal Lake by happy accident, he found work in the gold mine, and they started to build a house—and their dreams. Within a couple of years, they had a son...'

'You?'

'Yeah.'

'You must have been adorable,' Virginia said softly, captivated by the image of a dark-haired, blue-eyed infant that sprang to mind.

'Hardly!' His smile vibrated through his voice, causing the shadows to shift over the planes of his face. 'Born squawking and ready to take on the entire world, from all accounts.'

'I guess some things never change, then.'

Jordan's sideways glance of amusement quickly died as he continued, 'They thought they were all set for success. But just before I started school, the old man who'd hired my father stepped down and his son took over the mine.'

'Andrew Kent, *my* father.'

Jordan nodded. 'Your father. Things were never the same after that. There was a different sort of focus. The name of the game was not gainful employment for a town that depended on the mine for its livelihood, it was profit for the man at the top. A few years after that, my father developed asthma—fairly mild attacks, to begin with, that didn't slow him down all that much. But the dust in the mine irritated his lungs and eventually he had to take time off from work. Just a day or two here and there at first, but it was enough to draw him to Andrew Kent's displeased attention.

'Realizing that he stood to lose his job if he couldn't carry a full shift, Patrick asked to be assigned to other work. His schooling had been limited but he had a natural affinity for figures and thought he could be useful in the mine office, maybe with the accounts or something.' A flinty edge sharpened Jordan's tone. 'I guess he wasn't as smart as he thought.'

'What do you mean?'

'Andrew Kent wasted no time informing him that blue-collar labourers did not mingle with white-collar professionals. Patrick Caine would do well to remember his place, he was told, and if he didn't like where it took him, he was welcome to find work elsewhere—except, of course, there was no "elsewhere". The mine is the heartbeat of Opal Lake; it always has been. And my father had no choice but to stay where he was or face unemployment.

'His health worsened. By the time I was ten, he was reduced to working perhaps one shift out of four. I remember waking in the night and hearing him trying to breathe, an awful rasping wheeze that penetrated the paper-thin walls of the apartment where we were living. I used to lie there and count the seconds, terrified that he wouldn't breathe again. By then, the house my folks built when they first came to town had been sold to pay the bills. My mother scrubbed floors and took in sewing to make ends meet. After school and on weekends, I delivered newspapers and ran errands on a beat-up old bike that I rescued from the town dump.'

Virginia was appalled. 'But couldn't your father have retired on a disability pension? Certainly he'd have qualified.'

'Oh, come now, Highness!' The laughter that punctuated Jordan's reply was not kind. 'Disability pension? From whom? The benevolent Andrew Kent? You've got to be kidding!'

'Insurance, then? There must have been something.'

'I'm afraid not, my sweet innocent. Andrew Kent was bent on *making* money for his personal use, not *spending* it on outsiders. He had a certain lifestyle to maintain, after all. A mansion in which to entertain the rich and powerful; a wife to be dressed in the latest fashions from Europe; children to be sent to the most exclusive private schools. Important things beside which the health of one insignificant miner didn't amount to a hill of beans.'

Jordan steepled his fingers beneath his chin broodingly. 'So, Patrick kept on working, as best he could and when he could. Until, one day, he collapsed and was rushed to hospital by ambulance. He was hooked up to a respirator, fighting for his life, when J. D. Ellis, the mine manager, visited him there, sent by your father to relay the news that his services were no longer required. "Sorry, Pat," JD said, "boss's orders. Can't afford to carry a lame duck like you any longer."'

Virginia groaned quietly and sank her face into her hands, all too able to believe a situation which bore so clearly her father's unmistakably callous stamp. 'How did you manage then?'

'Hardly at all. When a man's stripped of his pride and reduced to begging, he loses the will to go on. My father never came home again.' Iordan drew a long, ragged breath. 'Patrick Caine worked for the Opal Lake Gold Mine for nearly fifteen years. When he died, the management sent a wreath of white chrysanthemums and a card signed by somebody we'd never heard of. The night after the funeral, I climbed the wall to your house and threw the wreath in the swimming pool.'

'Oh, God!' Virginia covered her mouth with her hands, tears pricking at her eyes. 'I remember that, but I had no idea what it signified.'

'Well, you do now,' Jordan flung out.

She couldn't bear to witness his pain. Through the haze of her tears, she reached for him, turned his face to hers, and traced the unhappy outline of his mouth. 'Oh, Jordan,' she said brokenly, 'I am so sorry, and so ashamed. No wonder you hate me. No wonder——'

'That's the whole trouble,' he said against her touch. 'Much as I wish I could, I find myself unable to hate you.'

Overcome by a disquieting urge to kiss away the hurt and grief he'd endured, she stroked the pure angle of his jaw, testing with the sensitive pads of her fingertips the day-old stubble of his beard. 'Yes, you do. I've seen it in your eyes and wondered why. I've heard it in your voice and tried to figure out what I'd said or done to provoke it.'

'As if you cared!' he said with a half-hearted return to his usual cynicism.

'But I did—I do,' she insisted, unable to prevent a solitary tear from rolling down her face. 'Against my better judgement, I let you hurt me with your remarks and insinuations. I wanted you to feel about me the way I feel about you.'

He grew very still and his voice was oddly hoarse as he asked, 'And how is that exactly, Virginia?'

How was she supposed to answer such a leading question? Averting her eyes from his searching gaze, she looked instead at his mouth. It was too close to hers, too sexy, and altogether too irresistible. 'Like this,' she whispered, settling on the only possible answer.

Her mouth felt as soft and sweetly uncertain as a petal shaken loose from a rose. Instinct had him rushing to capture it before it fell away and because he did, the outcome was as inevitable as a row of dominoes falling one after the other.

Somehow—barely—he'd withstood her pride, her aristocratic reserve, her delicious, unconscious sexuality. But her selfless grief disarmed him utterly. He took her in his arms and she felt . . . hollow. He could find no other word to fit the sense of her fragility at that moment, as if all the energy had been leached out of her by the reliving of their shared memories.

Acutely aware that he trod the knife-edge of a danger zone whose tolerance for fools was zero, Jordan made a last-ditch effort to retreat. There was such an artless innocence in the way she offered herself to him—not intentionally provocative, as she raised her arms and made her breasts rise full and sweet against her dress— but he knew a stab of desire that left him aching. And furious with himself.

He pulled away from her, adjusted his hold to resemble that of a parent comforting a child, and murmured into her hair, soft, soothing nothings meant to spell comfort.

Sensing his reluctance to press his advantage, she made a little sound, infinitely soft and quiescent. Generous. Trusting. He couldn't deal with it or her. She came weighted with too much responsibility and he carried enough already.

But then she lifted her face to his once more, brought her mouth back to his, and pressed her lips against his, again. And again. And his chance to escape was lost.

Desire gathered speed, like a train roaring through the night. Driving, devastating. Powerful, unstoppable. There was no turning back, no turning aside. Voracious and unpremeditated wanting had him crushing her to him in a fever of desire. Pure lunacy had him throwing aside the well-defended barricades behind which he'd protected his heart for so many years. And after that, he and she both were beyond salvation. He knew it and he despaired, even as he ravished her mouth with kisses that spelled his intent with probing, potent clarity.

She seemed to melt beneath his touch, managing somehow to flow into the empty hurting places he'd tried to ignore for too long. Blind to everything but his feelings, he sank with her to the mossy bank of the lily-pond.

He swept a hand up her sweetly curved body. Heard the swish of cotton as her skirt shimmied the length of her silk-smooth legs, the soft pop of a clasp and the sigh of lace. He tasted the warm scented arch of her throat and despaired anew as his body's desire to possess her raced ahead, leaving his brain befuddled at the starting post.

Not like this, he begged, on a last wave of disintegrating reason. But the plea was too little and much too late, and his clarity of mind too foggy with the demands of a craving dedicated to the gratification of its own delirious needs.

She was afraid. Not because her virginity was important to her but because it might be to him. If it were, he might feel compelled to stop and she thought she would die then from the raging white-hot fire uncoiling inside her.

Were they his hands or hers, rushing to remove clothing that seemed almost to shed itself in its anxiety to escape the blistering heat? His tortured lungs or hers gasping for breath?

She reached for him, blundering from the smooth curve of his ribs to the corrugated symmetry of his stomach. 'Jordan...where are you...?' she cried thinly.

'Here.' He hung poised above her, god-like. Golden with lamplight, burnished with night.

She slid her palms over his chest. 'Love me,' she beseeched, 'please...just this once...'

For a moment he hesitated, then sank down and possessed her with such exquisite, thrilling finesse that a whimper tore loose from her throat.

'Oh, Virginia...!' Overwhelmed by despair, a groan escaped him.

She knew that, given half a chance, he'd have left her trembling on the near side of paradise. She could not, *would* not, allow it. 'No, please,' she sighed.

For just a second, his heart slowed alarmingly. Or perhaps it was hers, or both of theirs, and they were dying. It didn't matter. Nothing mattered but that they know the glory hanging like a raindrop ready to fall; imminent, certain, and not quite close enough to catch. And then the life-beat began again, more frenzied, more urgent, communicating itself to their bones, their flesh, their souls. Propelling them in awesome harmony through some preordained ritual that sent them racing toward that crystal prize only to have it shatter as they captured it, and shower them with a thousand rainbows.

Gradually, the thunder died, allowing a hearing to the rest of the world: the musical fall of water from the stone fountain, the jubilant trill of a hermit thrush, Jordan's trembling, regretful sigh. And then, a deep, unnerving silence.

Dreading it, and afraid there was nothing she could do to subvert it, Virginia rushed to acknowledge it because she knew, with frightful conviction, what he would say if she let him be the first to break it. And she couldn't bear to have him rob her of her short-lived joy; better to throw it away herself.

'Why did we do this?' she asked, injecting a light-heartedness into the question designed to convey the idea that their making love hadn't been anything of great import to either one of them.

His reply fulfilled her worst expectations. 'Because,' he said bleakly, 'we let pity and compassion get in the way of sound judgement. We felt sorry for each other, Highness, and that is one hell of a poor reason for two responsible adults to make careless love.'

She bit down on her lip, hard enough to draw blood, but the pain didn't begin to equate that in her heart. 'Oh, well,' she said, with quavering, pathetic bravado, 'at least I'm rid of my chastity before its shelf-life expired. That's something, I suppose.'

He rolled to his feet in one swift, graceful move. 'Stop it!' he ordered, flinging on his clothes with angry haste. 'Cheap flippancy doesn't become you.'

Hurt and misery welled up, closing her throat in what promised to be an onslaught of tears to rival the Great Flood. Swallowing repeatedly, Virginia struggled for composure. Averting her face, she turned to the lily-pond and wished for nothing more than to submerge her head and leave it underwater until the last breath was choked from her beleaguered lungs.

'How long are you going to lie there like the Lady of the Lake?' Jordan snapped, knotting his tie with vicious flicks of his wrist. 'Get dressed, for God's sake, before someone comes looking for us.'

Curling on her side, she reached for the bundle of clothes he tossed at her and hugged them against her, horribly embarrassed by the damp trickle seeping over her thigh. 'I wish you would go back to the house ahead of me,' she murmured.

He favoured her with a cold smile. 'It's a bit late in the day for modesty.'

'But not too late for revulsion,' she was goaded into replying. 'Quite frankly, the sight of you is beginning to turn my stomach.'

'Well, what did you expect? That by condescending to kiss the toad, he'd turn into a prince?' Jordan snapped his collar into place and turned to go. 'Sorry to disappoint you, Highness, but what you see is what you got.'

And it's enough. You're all I'll ever want! she almost blurted out, and bit her lip a second time.

A deep inner sadness tore through her. I'm in love with him, she acknowledged at last, numb with the pain of it. Oh please, dear God, help me!

When she got back to the house, it was to find Jordan muttering his thanks to David and practically shoving his mother and son out of the front door in his haste to be gone before he had to confront the object of his indiscretion again. Certainly, of the three Caines, only Maria seemed glad to see her. Patrick was whining with fatigue and boredom, and Jordan...

Jordan flung her a glare full of regret, resentment, guilt and any number of other emotions except the one Virginia most wanted to see: a spark, however fleeting, of something approaching love or tenderness.

Ever the acute observer, Maria watched the exchange then fastened her gaze on Jordan with a sharp maternal perception that reduced even him to shuffling his feet and blushing faintly.

'Well,' David said, once the door had swung closed behind the visitors, 'what was all that about, sister dear?'

'I'm not sure I understand what you mean,' Virginia temporised, scrambling to deflect his curiosity.

She ought to have known better than to try to fool David. 'The tension that cut through the air cleaner than a hot knife through butter, for a start,' he replied, slipping a hand in the crook of her elbow and drawing her back toward the living-room. 'Not to mention the concern in Maria's voice when she thanked you for inviting her to tea, or the rumble of disgust in Jordan's when he muttered something about having taken up enough of our time. None of which, I might add, comes close to the aura of distress clinging to you that sharpens the scent of your perfume and has you breathing like a fish that by great mischance accidentally jumped clear of the water and can't find its way back into the bowl.'

'We talked about Father when we went outside,' she said, wretchedly aware that, up until now, she'd never felt the need to lie to her brother. They'd never kept secrets from each other, never been afraid to tell the plain, unvarnished truth, no matter how painful it might have been.

David found his way to the piano and idled through the opening bars of Beethoven's 'Moonlight Sonata'. 'You do realize you're in love with him, don't you?'

'In love with him?' Virginia scoffed, choosing to ignore the fact that she'd arrived at the same conclusion herself not too long ago. 'Don't be ridiculous, David. The man's cold and driven to succeed. Like Father. And, also like Father, unable to bond with his son who's not perfectly cast in his image. He's also insensitive, rude, sarcastic, moody, temperamental...'

She stopped, less because she'd run out of steam than to draw breath before launching into verse two. But Susan, who'd come into the room in time to hear the conversation, laughed and said, 'You're in love, all right.'

'No! I most certainly am not!'

'Rather badly, too, I'd say,' David added, swinging around on the piano bench and making room for Susan to sit beside him.

'You'll be telling me next that he feels the same way about me,' Virginia said plaintively.

'And well he might.' Unlike Susan, David looked sober. 'But Maria and I also found time to talk while

you were outside and the problem is, the man comes
with a lot of history, Virginia, a lot of baggage. Which
raises the question, how does he go about dealing
with another major complication in his already
complicated life?'

CHAPTER EIGHT

VIRGINIA got the answer midway through the following morning.

'Joey is looking for you, *cara*,' Maria panted, seeking her out in the ballroom where she was consulting with the painter on the final decorative touches to the ornate moulding surrounding the domed glass ceiling. 'He wants to see you in his office right away.'

'Probably to tell me I'm fired,' Virginia muttered under her breath.

Jordan was on the phone when she arrived at his door. He waved her to a seat on the other side of his ratty old plywood contraption of a desk and continued with his conversation, all the while scribbling notes on a pad. 'Implement the plan right away,' he ordered his listener. 'I want the benefits in place before the first shift clocks in... Absolutely. All dependents will be covered, regardless. And get me those figures on college bursaries a.s.a.p....'

Seizing the chance, Virginia studied him, determined to be objective in enumerating his flaws, which, she reminded herself, were legion. But all that talk about the harsh, revealing light of day was just so much rubbish where Jordan Caine was concerned. One look at that arrogant European profile, softened by eyes as blue as the Adriatic and a mouth so beautifully sensual it was small wonder that, even as a sixteen-year-old, she'd fallen victim to its erotic tug, and her heart was putty all over again. He wasn't perfect, not by a long shot; in fact, he was a rogue—but captivating and a man of conscience, for all that.

'How are you this morning?' he enquired, hanging up the receiver and jolting her out of her reverie.

'Perfectly well, thank you,' she replied evenly, loath to betray how deeply her affections had been embroiled in last night's exchange.

'Good,' he said, reaching behind him for the jacket slung over the back of his chair and fishing in one of its inside pockets. He withdrew a black paper bag embossed in silver with some name or other, and set it carefully in the middle of the desk top. 'I've reached a decision.'

'About what?'

'Us.' He tipped over the bag and let an egg-shaped silver jeweller's box fall out. 'I'm prepared to marry you.'

'Are you?' she managed, rendered almost speechless with shock and outrage.

'Yes.'

'Why?'

'You know why, so let's not belabour the point. We can announce our engagement at the Miners' Ball.' He poked the jeweller's box and sent it rolling over to her side of the desk. 'I went shopping for a ring this morning. Needless to say, my mother is over the moon at the news.'

'Is she?' Still too humiliated to retaliate with anything more complex than one or two word questions, Virginia stared at the gleaming silver egg and tried very hard not to lose her breakfast.

'Oh, yes. She had you earmarked as the perfect wife from the minute she set eyes on you. Don't you want to look at your ring?'

'No, thank you.'

'Why not? It's a two-and-a-half-carat stone, excellent colour and almost flawless.' He leaned across and snapped open the lid of the box. From within, embedded in black velvet, a marquise-cut diamond set in platinum winked up at her, its blue fire as coldly impersonal as its donor.

'I'm sure it is,' Virginia agreed, rallying slightly, 'and I hope that, one day, you find someone willing to wear it.'

For the first time, it seemed to occur to Jordan that she wasn't performing cartwheels of joy at the prospect of becoming his bride. 'If you prefer, we can change it for something else.'

'Not at all. It's a very nice piece of jewellery.'

'But?'

'But I don't want to marry you,' she told him, adding disdainfully, 'thank you very much.'

His gaze narrowed. 'I see. It isn't the ring that's not good enough, it's me.'

Virginia didn't reply. What was the point? He couldn't give her what she wanted, and she couldn't accept what he was willing to give.

'You might be pregnant, you know.'

'I might be, but it's not likely.'

He drew a long, perplexed breath. 'Damn it, woman, I know you were a virgin and that what I allowed to happen last night is hard to forgive, but I'm not completely without conscience. I'm willing to do the honourable thing.'

'I'm not willing to accept charity.'

'Oh, for Pete's sake!' He slammed his palm resoundingly on the plywood desk and sent the open jeweller's box, ring and all, into a dazzling spin. 'Look, we're mature adults. Admittedly, it isn't an ideal situation, but if we work at it, we can make a go of it. Patrick needs a mother, Maria longs for a daughter——'

'And you?' Virginia interrupted, glaring at him. 'What do you need, Jordan?'

'I—I... Damn it, I need ...'

'Someone to assuage your sexual appetite,' she supplied witheringly. 'And, with your aversion to settling for other people's leavings, I fit the bill very well.'

His blue eyes blazed with frustration. 'Where the hell did that remark come from?'

'From taking on the job of redecorating this house. As I recall, you wanted no part of anything the previous owners had left behind, so I suppose it makes a perverted sort of sense that you'd feel the same way about the woman you deign to choose for a wife.' It cost Virginia dearly, but she managed to lift her shoulders in a shrug weighted with contempt. 'And the fact that, in addition to my laughably outdated virginity, I also have an impeccable pedigree no doubt adds tremendously to my value.'

The thoughtful, painfully honest look he brought to bear on her shamed her and almost had her making a dash for the door. 'Pedigree played no part in what happened between us last night, Virginia, and if you thought it did then either you're a fool or a very good actress.'

'I think we both agree that what happened between us last night was a mistake,' she said, ignoring the shaft of pain that lanced her heart. 'I see no reason to compound it by entering into what would surely be a marriage of the utmost inconvenience for both of us. And now, if that is all, I would like to return to my work.'

Certain he'd be as glad to be rid of her as she was anxious to escape, she rose from her seat and prepared to make as dignified an exit as she could muster.

'Not yet, damn it! This subject is not closed.' Jordan sprang out of his chair, baffled, angry, slightly ashamed for some inexplicable reason, and—oh, what the hell!— *disappointed*. 'Do you have any idea,' he continued, planting both hands on the desk and leaning over her, 'what it cost me to propose to you like this?'

'Apart from several thousand dollars for the ring? Oh, yes,' she replied, in that saintly, supercilious tone she held in reserve for those times when louts like him forgot to tug respectfully on their forelocks. 'I'm sure you gave it a great deal of thought. You probably walked the floor all night, polishing every word.'

'So that's what this is really all about,' he said, sinking back into his seat. 'You don't like the way I went about it.'

'No, I don't,' she assured him, her dainty little nose wrinkling with distaste. 'Not in the least.'

'For crying out loud, Virginia, do you think I do this sort of thing every other day and that I'm so well-versed in the finer points that I can rattle off the words without a second thought?'

She didn't answer. Instead, she pinched her lips together, as though he'd made her a gift of something unspeakably vulgar, and clenched her hands in her lap.

'Don't tell me you want me on bended knee, begging, and pledging happy-ever-after if only you'll honour me with an acceptance?' he scoffed. 'If so, you can whistle in the wind till we're both confined to rockers in an old folks' home. I've gone the so-called traditional route once, already, and all it brought me was a load of grief.'

'You have my condolences,' she chirped, fluttering her eyelashes and looking about as sympathetic as a nurse about to stab his backside with a long, sharp needle.

'The church is right, you know,' he went on, not quite sure why he was pursuing a subject neither of them was particularly enjoying. 'Marriage isn't something to be entered into lightly or unadvisedly; it's something to be approached with caution, logic and the utmost realism.'

She bent her attention on her hands that still lay clenched in her lap, and murmured accommodatingly, 'Of course.'

'Furthermore, I'm not about to insult your intelligence by making protestations of undying love when we both know better. What counts in marriage is mutual respect and liking. That other stuff is just...'

She looked up then, her luminous gray eyes enormous in her delicate face, and fixed her gaze unwaveringly on his.

'Just...' he swallowed and pressed one hand to his chest, wondering what he'd eaten for breakfast to be giving him such god-awful indigestion at this hour of the morning '... a load of hogwash,' he finished lamely.

'Absolutely. May I go now?'

'Hell, yes,' he grumbled, unaccountably put out by her reaction. 'Don't let me keep you from more important matters.'

'I won't.'

She rose gracefully from her chair and swayed to the door where she paused, a vision of full-skirted turquoise elegance. 'By the way,' she ordained regally, 'with the exception of your bedroom and this office, the house is just about finished. If I'm to execute suitable changes in here, you'll have to find somewhere else to conduct your affairs for the next little while, which you will undoubtedly find very inconvenient, but I'm afraid it simply can't be helped.'

'Since I have to be away on business for the next two weeks, it happens to be perfectly convenient. Otherwise,' he continued, feeling compelled to remind her that, even though she'd turned down his proposal, he was still the boss, '*you* would have to rearrange your schedule to accommodate *me*.'

She raised her delicate eyebrows, gave a little flounce of her head, and exited the room, the restraint with which she closed the door spelling utter defiance for his authority.

Just once, he thought savagely, he'd like to provoke her into telling him to get stuffed. If nothing else, it would put them on a more equal footing.

The house was horribly empty without him, although his presence dogged Virginia as she went to work on those rooms that comprised his personal domain.

Still, she managed to take care of his office-cum-library with reasonable efficiency, settling without too much difficulty on a thorough cleaning of the bevelled glass-fronted bookcases. Hand-rubbed to satiny perfection, the fine old rosewood panelling that curved along the shelves and around the perimeter of the room to embrace door and windows in six-inch mouldings required no further embellishment.

The floor she covered with a Turkish rug whose rich reds echoed the burgundy swags over the stained-glass windows, and completed the décor with a fine antique library desk that might have been made to go with the swivel chair Jordan had brought with him the day he'd taken possession of the house.

His bedroom, however, was another matter entirely. She dawdled there for half a day, ignoring the decisions at which she and Jordan had arrived regarding a fitting décor, and flitting from one whimsical idea to another. She was painfully aware that, but for her pride and a certain naïve idealism, it could have been her bedroom, too.

If it were, she decided, settling into a corner of the padded window seat and giving free rein to her imagination, she'd discard the navy striped bedspread and draperies which had been the original choice, and forget the pale gray walls that made the place look more like a prison cell than a home within a home.

In their place, she'd paint the walls a deep and restful blue. The bed she'd pile high with snow-white duvets and pillows, and cover the tall windows with yards of sheer white draperies that would flutter and swirl in the breeze like morning mist over the lake. For summer days when the sun beat in too intensely, she'd hang slatted white blinds next to the glass; and for winter nights, when the wind howled and the snow crept up the outside sills, a fireplace in the corner.

She'd fling a thick white rug on the wide maple floorboards and forget the gentleman's wardrobe and angular brass bed that Jordan had approved when she'd first presented him with her ideas. Instead, she'd take tomorrow off to attend the estate auction that she'd seen advertised in Halford, and bid on the maple bedroom suite pictured in the catalogue. From the carved roses rimming the high headboard to the bow-fronted chest of drawers and dressing-table, it was a relic from a bygone age when rooms like those in the mansion were designed to accommodate such grandiose proportions.

But her succumbing to its charm would almost certainly invoke Jordan's abiding displeasure. Unless, of course, she managed to enchant him with the sheer romance of it all.

There was an old-fashioned black telephone perched at the other end of the window seat. Almost absently, she pulled it on to her lap and dialled a number. 'It's Virginia Kent,' she said, when her supplier answered. 'There's been a change of plan. Please hold tomorrow's delivery for the Caine mansion until you hear from me. I'll let you know within a couple of days whether or not we still need it.'

Maria was very unhappy. 'No, *cara*,' she wailed, when Virginia told her, firmly but kindly, that under no circumstances would she attend the Miners' Ball. 'First I am banished from my kitchen, then my son growls at me there will be no wedding after all. Now you tell me I must face all those strangers alone. I cannot do it. *You* cannot do it to me. Please!'

'I'll help you prepare for it. We'll have everything organized and ready to go. All you'll have to do is dress up and smile. The rest will take care of itself.'

'But you promised you'd be there with me.'

'Actually,' Virginia said, 'I didn't. When you come right down to it, Jordan coerced me and tricked you into believing that was so.'

'What does it matter how or why? It does not change how I feel. I am out of my depth, Virginia, with everything.'

'Then you must let Jordan know that. Tell him you aren't comfortable acting as his hostess and that it's his responsibility to take charge once guests begin to arrive.'

'*Tell* Joey?' Maria repeated. 'Even at the best of times, he is not a man to take kindly to orders but now, since his fine plans to marry you fell apart, he is impossible.

Are you sure, Virginia,' she continued earnestly, 'that there is no chance for you and him?'

'Not as things presently stand.'

Maria watched her closely for a moment, then said, 'But you wish it were not so, I can tell. There is such sadness in your voice, Virginia, and such a special look in your eyes. I think perhaps you could love him, given time.'

'Time isn't going to change his reasons for proposing in the first place, Maria, or the way he went about doing it—as if it were just another piece of business to be dealt with as speedily and efficiently as possible.'

'Ah, so that is it!' Maria sat down and folded her hands in her lap. 'Virginia, *cara*, perhaps there is something I should explain. My Joey, he is not always wise in the way he does things but that does not mean his heart is not in the right place. He looks for perfection first in himself and, if he thinks it is not there, he hides his pain and pretends he does not care.'

'He wasn't hiding anything from me,' Virginia said wretchedly. 'He made it quite clear his heart played no part in his offer to marry me. In fact, his indifference leaves me so profoundly unhappy that I've found myself envying his ex-wife. At least *she* stirred him to feel something. In the beginning, it might even have been love.'

'No,' Maria said, and sighed. 'When he was a boy, my son used to come home with rocks that sparkled with "pyrite" I think it was called. It would make us rich, he used to say, because he was too young to know it was only fool's gold. He made the same mistake when he married Penelope. At first it might have looked like the real thing, but it turned out to be fool's love. Now he is all grown up, Virginia, and he knows the difference.'

'I'm afraid that doesn't change the way I feel, Maria. Jordan expects the best from everyone around him, including me, no matter how hard it might be to give it. I won't settle for less from him.'

'Why is it that, no matter how much we have, we always want more?' Maria shrugged sadly. 'At last, this house begins to look like a home. The mine is nearly ready to open and my Joey sees one of his dreams come true. Patrick is acting more like a normal little boy instead of a frightened shadow. I have so much to make me happy...' She rolled soulful eyes heavenward, then cast a sly glance at Virginia to make sure she had her full attention before making her final pitch. 'Except for two things. The first you cannot yet give me, and that I accept. The other—one evening, a few hours only— you will not give me.'

'Maria,' Virginia protested, half laughing, 'I don't even have a dress that would be suitable! I haven't been to a function like this in years and it's much too late to order anything now. The Miners' Ball is only ten days away.'

'And if that were the only obstacle?' Maria's liquid brown gaze fixed itself hopefully on Virginia.

Resistance beginning to crumble, Virginia sighed. 'Oh, I suppose I'd consider it, but only as a favour to you.'

'Then it is done!' Maria clapped her plump hands gleefully and did a sort of pirouette around her little sitting-room. 'I will start sewing tomorrow—at your house, if that is all right with you? It will be easier to do the fitting that way, you understand?'

'All right, whatever's most convenient. But, Maria, I don't want to impose on you.'

'Impose? Hah! You are doing me a favour. I am *happy* to make a dress for you, Virginia. For the first time in many days, I feel useful again.' She reached for a pencil and notepad. 'I will have Signor Thurston bring my sewing machine in the car when he drives Patrick down to play with Tramp. But before then, *cara*, you and I must go shopping for pretty material. This afternoon, yes?'

Virginia shrugged. It was all the agreement Maria needed.

*　　*　　*

When Jordan got back six days later, his house was finished and his mother more cheerful than he'd seen her in months. 'Hey, there've been a few changes since I left,' he remarked, dumping his suitcase in the front hall and flinging an arm around Maria's shoulders as he surveyed his office. 'This looks pretty nice.'

From her vantage point on the upper landing, Virginia was able to observe him without being seen. With the knot in his tie loosened and the cuffs of his pale gray shirt rolled back, he looked tired and elegantly rumpled. The yearning to run down and welcome him with a kiss, to smooth the hair back from his brow and exchange a private glance that promised, 'Later!' left her aching. If only he'd proposed differently; if only she hadn't been so quick to turn him down. If only...

Emerging from his office, Jordan turned toward the stairs, his arm still slung affectionately over his mother's shoulder. 'So, Momma, what have you been up to while I was gone?'

Virginia stepped back into Maria's sitting-room and pretended to busy herself tallying numbers for the caterer though, in fact, she really was holding her breath, waiting for the axe to fall when Jordan saw his new bedroom.

'Virginia and I are working together on the final details for the Ball,' Maria said, with a judicious blend of honesty and deceit, since most of her time had been spent working on Virginia's gown.

They had reached the landing. Virginia could see their shadows cast by the late afternoon sun across the wall just outside the door to Maria's suite.

Jordan's voice had a peculiar timbre to it when he asked, 'Virginia's here?'

'Yes. And Patrick is in his room, playing quietly for once. What a change in a boy, Joey! You would be so proud to see him with David's dogs.'

Jordan's tone, which had almost returned to normal, faded a little as he replied, indicating he'd turned away from his mother's room and was heading toward his own. 'David's idea's working, is it?'

'Oh, definitely!' Maria's laughter floated down the hall. 'More and more, your son reminds me of you when you were that age. He's decided it's time to visit the mine with his papa.'

'Well, that's great. Maybe I'll take him with me tomorrow morning, unless you've made other——'

From the abrupt silence that followed, Virginia guessed he'd reached the threshold of his room. She waited for him to finish the sentence he'd started. Or to begin another one. Or to let out a howl of outrage.

Instead, the silence continued unbroken. Even Maria's stream of chit-chat appeared to have run dry. The house was utterly quiet, except for the heavy thud of Virginia's heart. Until the measured tread of Jordan's footsteps split the silence as he came back along the upper hall and paused in the doorway of the sitting room where she sat feigning absorption over the guest list.

She refused to look up. Refused to acknowledge him at all. Let him be the first to break the silence, she thought defiantly.

She felt the air around her stir a little, as though a faint breeze had disturbed it. She sensed the shadow at her back. And still she wasn't prepared for the long, tanned fingers that reached over her shoulder and plucked the pencil from her visibly shaking hands. 'Come with me, Highness,' he breathed in her ear.

She went with him, docile as a sleepwalker and just about as comatose. He led her by the wrist past a wide-eyed Maria, who pressed herself against the wall to let them by, and brought her to a halt in the doorway to his room.

The filmy white drapes shimmered in the sun and floated on gentle drafts of air from the open window. The carved roses on the headboard of the maple bed peeked saucily over the mound of snowy pillows scattered on the puffy duvet.

On a side table, a vase of white roses stood sentinel next to what surely rated as Virginia's ultimate folly in this whole affair: a late-Victorian fainting couch, upholstered in blue velvet, which she'd seen for the first time when it was hauled up on the block at the same auction that had brought her the bedroom suite. She had fallen in love with its flowing curves and elegant legs, bid on it heedlessly, and ended up owning it.

The best she could offer in defence of her impetuosity was that, if Jordan didn't want it, she'd gladly take it off his hands. But she hoped he'd want to keep it; it might have been made for the room.

Jordan was staring at her. She could feel his gaze, blue and penetrating, boring into her. She desperately needed to swallow and knew, if she did, that he'd notice and deduce, correctly, that beneath her serene façade she was plagued with apprehension at what she'd done. Why, she wondered belatedly, had she arbitrarily elected to ignore Jordan's choice of a plain and simple effect, and settled instead on this other, whimsical décor?

He propelled her into the middle of the room and spun her lightly around so that she could observe it from every angle. 'Do you want to tell me,' he inquired gently, 'what possessed you to make my bedroom look like something from the set of Rudolf Valentino's last movie?'

'Don't you like it?' she whispered.

He rocked back on his heels and chewed his lip meditatively. He let his gaze roam the four walls, the floor, the windows, the bed. Especially the bed. 'Do you?'

'I think it's very...romantic. Without being frilly or fussy.'

'*Romantic*?'

'Yes.'

'What made you settle on *romance*, Virginia? Did you think I needed a little romance in my life, is that it?'

She quailed before his gaze. 'Perhaps.'

He stepped closer and tilted her chin with his finger. 'And if I said I agreed, would that make you reconsider your summary dismissal of my marriage proposal?'

There it was, that second chance so seldom granted a person to do things over, differently. She thought about saying, Yes, and I think you're right. We could make a go of marriage if we worked at it. Or, if that seemed too eager, simply, Yes, and let him take things from there. But pride ran stronger than courage. 'The thought never crossed my mind,' she said stiffly.

He stepped back, a chill gleam in his eye. 'Of course not. How foolish of me to think it would.' The finger that had tipped her chin so temperately yanked savagely at the knot in his tie. 'What about the arrangements for the Midsummer Festival and Miners' Ball? I trust you haven't seen fit to make a lot of unauthorized changes there, too?'

'Not at all. Everything is going exactly as you requested it except for one or two snags that still have to be ironed out.'

'With less than a week before the big day, that's one or two snags too many,' he informed her high-handedly. 'I told you before, I won't tolerate anything less than the best.'

Maria showed up early at Virginia's house the next day. 'This morning, Joey has taken Patrick to see how the mine works,' she said, her eyes gleaming with mischief, 'and he's planning to do the same thing tomorrow morning, too. So, I am here by myself, with nothing to occupy me but the making of your beautiful gown.'

'But you should take the time off for yourself,' Virginia protested. 'I know well enough how tired you are by the end of a full day with Patrick. Good grief, he wears me out with all his energy, and I'm only twenty-nine!'

But Maria brushed aside her concern. 'And what should I do instead?' she scoffed. 'Sit in the back seat of a car too big for one person, and let a stranger drive me around town? Or wait until Mrs Douglass, the fancy new cook, turns her back so that I can creep into *my* kitchen and make a decent cup of coffee? Hah! I would rather be here, doing what I love to do, and enjoying conversation with David and Susan. At least with them I don't feel as if I'm a prisoner.'

'How does Jordan feel about you making me a dress?' Virginia asked uneasily.

An uncommonly sneaky smile lit up Maria's face. 'He does not know, *cara*. And as people say in this country, what he does not know does not hurt him.'

Although she agreed in principle, Virginia had no wish to heap Jordan's wrath on Maria's kindly head. 'If this is going to cause trouble between you and your son, Maria, I'd just as soon you didn't——'

'Don't say it!' Maria held up an imperious hand. 'No, I will not hear it. I make the dress and I do it because it gives me pleasure, it is as simple as that. This morning, Joey has taken Patrick with him to the mine, so we are safe. By tomorrow, I shall be finished and Joey need never be the wiser.'

'What if he decides to drop Patrick off here to play with Tramp?' Virginia pointed out. 'I heard you tell him yesterday how well the two of them are doing and he just might decide to come and see for himself.'

'I thought of that, and...' Maria looked mildly embarrassed. 'Well, *cara*, I took a small liberty. I suggested that, just for this afternoon, we bring Tramp up to our house. I hope you don't mind?'

'No. But I'm surprised Jordan agreed. He made it clear enough that he didn't want a dog racing around the place during the renovation and, if anything, it's an even worse time now, with the Festival and Ball so close. The tent's going up on the south lawn today, so the place will be crawling with workmen again.'

Maria's smile widened gleefully. 'Ah, but Joey does not know that. And he is very pleased to be able to spend the entire day with his son and still be near his office to

take all his important phone calls.' She patted Virginia's
hand comfortingly. 'Do not look so worried, *cara*! It is
just a little white lie and it is only for today.'

Over the last few weeks, Virginia had noticed a de-
terioration in Maria, as if the vitality were being drained
out of her. As Patrick had blossomed into greater in-
dependence and the house had neared completion, her
energy had dwindled proportionately and been replaced
by a listless acceptance of a life she didn't particularly
like but couldn't be bothered to change.

It had reminded Virginia of her own mother's decline.
In theory, illness had claimed Zoe Kent's life when she
was in her early forties. But Virginia had known that,
despite a background of wealth and privilege, the
emotional devastation brought about by her unhappy
marriage had depleted her mother's resilience and left
her too exhausted to fight back. It had been easier to
give up.

In Maria's case, the root of the problem was more
insidious but the end result could be the same. Jordan's
intentions, though good, were misguided. He was in
danger of killing his mother with kindness.

Since she'd started sewing Virginia's gown, though,
Maria had seemed better. Some of the sparkle that had
been so much in evidence when Virginia had first met
her was back. And so, although Virginia's instincts told
her things weren't going to work out quite as smoothly
as Maria predicted, she chose not to listen.

And learned the hard way what a mistake that was.

CHAPTER NINE

IT HAD been a long time since Jordan had felt so contented. Not sublimely happy—that was for fools and children—but, for a man who was, in his mother's words, 'too impatient, too demanding', today came as close to perfection as he could ask.

Except for the most urgent matters, he'd put business on the back burner until tomorrow and spent a satisfying morning showing off his son to the men at the mine, and showing off the mine to his son.

When they got back home, they'd shared an excellent lunch, served to them on the patio by Mrs Douglass, their new cook. Now, with Patrick safely down for a nap, the afternoon stretched ahead, and Jordan had nothing to do but relax and enjoy it. He couldn't remember the last time he'd felt able to afford such luxury. Beguiled by the sparkling pool, he changed into swimming trunks, determined that, when Patrick awoke, he'd get him in the water and give him his first swimming lesson.

Thinking of the changes that had taken place in his son, Jordan smiled. Almost overnight the kid had blossomed into an exuberant five-year-old dynamo, full of curiosity for the world about him. Some might call it vanity—and he supposed he'd have to agree that it was—but he had revelled in Patrick's limitless appetite for stories of Jordan's exploits when he'd been young. It did a man's ego a world of good to know that, for a little while at least, he was a hero in his son's eyes.

Maria, too, appeared to have accepted her new lifestyle with equanimity. Jordan knew it hadn't been easy for her at first. He'd heard her sneaking down to the kitchen in the middle of the night, had seen the light shining in her room until the small hours, and knew the insomnia she'd suffered when he was a child had returned with a vengeance. But the dejection that had lined her face had lifted in the last little while. She'd recouped some of her zest and the laughter was back in her eyes.

And as if all that weren't enough, he had the satisfaction of knowing that seventy-five per cent of the mine had been restored to safety; enough that, starting next week, a full complement of eight hour shifts would begin to roll. Most of the men idled by Ted Connaught's feckless ways would be back at work.

Raising the last of his lunchtime beer in a toast, he congratulated himself. The Midsummer Festival and Miners' Ball couldn't have been better timed. Everything was going his way—except, of course, for *her*.

At the thought of Virginia, his mood changed so suddenly that it was as if a cloud had sailed across the sun, darkening the sky.

Why had she to intrude on this moment of pleasure? he wondered irritably, then, with a fine disregard for logic, followed that question with another. And why the hell wasn't she here now, with his mother, looking after last-minute details for the weekend's festivities?

'Watch what you're doing!' he called, venting his annoyance on the men erecting a huge marquee down on the lawn. 'You've got those guy ropes so close to the pool deck, we'll be having people tripping and falling in the water.'

The crew muttered to themselves but did their best to accommodate him. Unlike Virginia who, obdurate as usual, hovered in his mind despite his best efforts to evict her.

To be fair, he owed her a lot. She'd performed wonders on his mausoleum of a house. He'd realized for some time that the true mark of her skill lay in the superb judgement with which she'd assessed his needs, then combined them with her good taste to produce a result that was as comfortable as it was elegant. Except for his bedroom which—oddly and despite her extravagant changes—struck him as too bare. As though some vital element of warmth or life were missing from its décor. Or, perhaps more accurately, as though the ghost of her presence were knocking at the door, begging to be allowed entry.

'What the hell——!' He swore in contemptuous distaste for his frailty as images of her pervaded his mind so vividly that, inevitably, a stirring physical response followed. He was sovereign of all he surveyed, all right— except his own body!

Next, he'd be convincing himself that he'd gone looking for an excuse to propose to her, or that there'd been more involved than runaway lust the night he'd seduced her. He must have had too much sun! Time for a swim to cool off his brain.

He'd covered perhaps ten laps when Virginia and his mother arrived on the scene. Patrick followed behind, accompanied by a large black and tan German shepherd, and screeched to a halt at the edge of the pool.

'Hey,' Jordan scolded, raking back his hair, 'you know the rules, kiddo. No playing near the water without a life-jacket.'

'It's too hot to wear that old thing,' Patrick informed him, skipping gleefully out of reach as his father hauled himself to the pool deck and tried to catch him.

'Little toad!' Jordan muttered in token protest, but he couldn't help grinning. He'd far rather his son were a rascal than the cowering child who'd first come to Opal Lake.

'I gather that's the famous Tramp,' he remarked, strolling over to where the women had settled themselves at a table shaded by a sun umbrella on the patio.

'Yes,' Virginia said rather coolly, not deigning to look up from her task of shuffling papers and ticking off various items.

She wore a strappy little sundress that left her shoulders and arms delectably bare. Vibrantly conscious of her perfume, he leaned over her chair. 'What's that you're working on?'

'Final numbers for the caterers. Maria, don't forget you have to go into Halford tomorrow at the latest, to pick up your outfits. There won't be time on Saturday.'

'Outfits?' Jordan echoed in mock horror. 'You mean there's more than one? What are you doing, Virginia, turning my mother into a clothes horse?'

'One gown is hardly enough to see her through a full twelve hours of hostessing,' she informed him curtly. 'She needs one outfit for the afternoon and another for the evening.'

'Well, hey, I was just teasing.' Taken aback by her chilly manner, Jordan fended Virginia off with both hands. 'Have you had lunch?'

'Yes, thank you. Your mother and I ate at my house before we came up here.'

'Well, then, may I get you something cool to drink? It's pretty warm again this afternoon.'

'Nothing for me, thanks. You're paying me to work, not socialize.'

'I know that,' he replied, his restored good temper souring a little in the face of her unyielding reserve. 'But that doesn't mean you're chained to the wall and obliged to subsist on stale bread and water.'

She lifted her head and accorded him a brief stare. 'In that case,' she said politely, 'a glass of iced tea would be very nice.'

'Fine,' he said, thoroughly irritated, with her for being so stand-offish, and with himself for giving a damn. 'Some iced tea would be very nice,' he mimicked, poking his head in the kitchen door and relaying the message to Mrs Douglass.

'Hey, Dad, watch me,' Patrick yelled, fearlessly retrieving a ball from the dog's mouth and flinging it across the lawn.

'I'm watching,' he replied, swabbing a towel over his chest.

Maria beamed indulgently as Patrick rolled around on the grass while the animal circled him playfully. 'You are pleased, Joey, to see your son so happy?'

'Yeah, Momma, I'm pleased. Who wouldn't be? He's changed—for the better. I wouldn't have believed it could happen so quickly, or that the dog could make such a difference. I owe your brother a debt of gratitude,' Jordan added, turning to Virginia and taking another stab at softening her mood.

She inclined an aristocratic little nod in his direction without missing a beat in her work. 'Maria, do you have the florist's order handy?'

His mother rummaged through her own sheaf of papers. 'It must be in my sitting-room,' she decided, bustling toward the house. 'I will go and look.'

Once she'd gone, Patrick's shrieks were the only sound to disturb the peace of the afternoon. Finally, Jordan could stand it no longer. 'I want to go over a few things with Virginia,' he told his son. 'If you'll go play somewhere else for a while and keep the noise down to a dull roar, I'll take you swimming later on.'

He waited until Patrick obligingly zoomed away under the trees, then turned back to her. 'I don't know why you're the one sulking,' he said, having no choice but to address the crown of her head since she continued to pore over her precious lists as if her life depended on them. 'I'm the one who had his ring tossed back in his face.'

'Yes,' she agreed snottily. 'And the wonder of it is, you still can't figure out why.'

'Oh, I figured it out, all right. You wanted me to lie and say it was love that made me do it, but I've got news for you, Highness. We plebs don't try to cover up the flaws in our relationships with a lot of fancy window-dressing. We prefer to see them for what they are and work on making them better.'

'Somehow, I don't think your mother would agree with you. From what she's told me, I'm pretty sure she married for love and never regretted it, despite the hardships.'

'I see.' He settled in the chair vacated by his mother and hitched it closer to Virginia's. 'So, what you're saying is that you don't think marriage can work unless the people involved are in love, is that it?'

'Not necessarily,' she replied, shuffling her own chair a few inches further away as though he were contagious. 'I'm sure there've been many successful partnerships based on other things. I just happen to be one of those people who believe in marrying for love and I'm not willing to settle for a shabby imitation of the real thing just to soothe your wounded pride, so please stop harping on the subject.'

'You know,' he said, ticked off beyond measure by her aloof uninterest in him when it took every scrap of control for him to keep his hands off her sun-kissed shoulders, 'you weren't so all-fired indifferent to me the night we made love. In fact, if I'd proposed then, instead of waiting until the next morning, I'm willing to bet you'd have said yes.'

She sniffed haughtily but couldn't disguise the delicious flush that ran up her neck to her face. Encouraged, he leaned so close that his lips were practically touching her hair. 'I don't think you find my attentions nearly as offensive as you'd have me believe, Highness,' he whispered in her ear.

Driven beyond endurance, Virginia rolled up her papers and swatted him with the same vigour that she'd have attacked a mosquito bent on biting a chunk out of her flesh.

Jordan was too close, too sexy and altogether too naked. And she was no more able to cope with that now, at twenty-nine, than she had been at sixteen when he'd flooded her adolescent innocence with strange longings.

She hadn't drawn an easy breath since she'd come out to the patio and found him emerging from the pool, his torso gleaming with water and that pathetic excuse of a swimsuit clinging by a thread to his lean hips. Tall and graceful, he was a tailor's dream. Broad across the shoulders, narrow at the waist, long legs tautly muscled, and the whole swathed in smooth olive skin.

Possessed by a wholly unreasonable joy at his persistence, it was all she could do not to give in to the urge to fling her arms around him and tell him that he was right, that she found him utterly charming and adorable. But she'd die before she let him see how affected she was by his attentions, so she swatted him a second time, sharply, just to let him know she wasn't about to be swayed by an expanse of tanned male chest or a smile that would have beguiled Medusa.

'Oho!' he chortled, making a grab for her wrist. 'Have I struck a nerve?'

Heaven only knew what might have occurred next if a refined, disapproving contralto hadn't chosen that moment to enquire, 'Jordan? Can that be you?'

He sprang bolt upright as if he'd been stung on the behind by a particularly vicious wasp. Following his gaze, Virginia found herself being assessed by a woman whose face was half-hidden behind an enormous pair of designer sunglasses. She wore a Calvin Klein two-piece suit of white silk, accessorised with black alligator shoes and bag. A wide-brimmed black straw hat covered her strawberry blonde head.

Jordan's reply was hardly gracious. 'Marguerite? Where the hell did you come from?' he demanded, casting a wary glance around as if he expected a broomstick to materialize out of thin air.

The woman stretched her mouth in a thin smile. 'Gracious as ever, I see. You haven't changed, my dear, despite your impressive setting.'

'What do you want, Marguerite?' The question shot from Jordan's lips with matching contempt. Tense as a gladiator confronting a lion, he stood with feet planted apart and hands hanging loosely at his sides.

'I have come to see my grandson, since you seem disinclined to allow him to visit Carstairs and me, despite our repeated invitations to you to do so,' the woman declared regally.

'And I explained when I replied that it's too soon for any of that,' Jordan said. 'He's only just beginning to adjust to living here with me. I'm afraid you'll have to——'

'Before you threaten to show me the door, let me remind you that we never once denied you access to Patrick during the nearly two years we took care of him for you so that you could pursue your career. It doesn't seem too much to ask for similar consideration in return, especially since reasonable visitation privileges are well within our grandparental rights.' She reached gracefully into her large black handbag and withdrew a folded document. 'And just in case you're tempted to be obstructive, I have taken the precaution of acquiring a court order to that effect.'

Jordan scowled. 'You know what you can do with your court order,' he informed her savagely, and, just in case she wasn't sure she did, went on to tell her in precise anatomical detail.

Even with the sunglasses covering the top half of her face, Virginia could tell the woman's eyebrows rose in amused disdain. Her perfectly lipsticked mouth stretched in another parody of a smile. 'One can take the boy out of the gutter,' she purred, 'but one can never quite take the gutter out of the boy. I can't wait to see the effect such an excellent role model is having on my grandson.'

'I'm not letting you within a mile of Patrick——' Jordan began, and Virginia knew that she had to step in to save him from himself.

'Until we've offered you some refreshment.' Rising to her feet and extending her hand, she rushed to effect a little damage control. 'How do you do? I'm Virginia Kent.'

'Are you indeed?' the woman replied, quite openly scanning Virginia from the top of her head to the soles of her sandalled feet. 'And might I ask where you fit into this unappetizing scenario?'

Bristling with rage, Jordan launched another attack. 'Not that it's any of your business, but Virginia is my——'

'Fiancée,' Virginia said, amazing herself as much as the other two with her rash announcement. 'And you, of course, are Jordan's former mother-in-law. Won't you please have a seat?'

'Thank you.' Marguerite Winslow sank into one of the chairs, visibly dumbfounded by Virginia's news. 'I had no idea that Jordan planned to marry again,' she said, removing her glasses.

Jordan leaned over to plant a saucy kiss on Virginia's cheek. 'Neither had I,' he declared, *sotto voce*. 'When did you change your mind?'

'We became engaged only a short time ago,' Virginia told Mrs Winslow with a smile and, under the guise of patting him on the arm, gave Jordan a somewhat unkind pinch.

Mrs Winslow was too occupied with other matters to notice. 'Is that why you aren't wearing his ring?' she enquired suspiciously.

'No,' Virginia said. 'I have a lovely ring but it was too large so Jordan took it back to the jeweller to be altered. Didn't you, darling?'

'Yes, darling,' he said, the gleam in his eye proclaiming his growing enjoyment of the whole charade. 'In fact, I got a call this morning to say it was ready, so I picked it up while I was in town. Let me go in and get it.'

Virginia hooked her arm in his, not about to be left alone with this pirhana of a woman. 'While you're doing that, I'll get us some fresh iced tea—unless you'd prefer something else, Mrs Winslow?'

'Perrier with a twist of lime would suit me better,' she said, tucking her glasses into an embroidered case and surveying the garden. 'And I would like to see Patrick sooner rather than later. I have travelled quite a long way, you know.'

Virginia nodded. 'Of course. I'll find him and bring him out, since I'm sure you don't have too long before you have to leave again.'

'On the contrary,' Marguerite Winslow replied. 'I accompanied Carstairs, my husband, to Vancouver, where he expects to be tied up on business matters until the middle of next week, so I plan to stay in Opal Lake several days. I presume there's a decent hotel somewhere close by?'

'Not really,' Jordan informed her cheerfully. 'This is a mining town, not Cap d'Antibes.'

She smiled back with malicious radiance. 'Then I'll have to stay here, won't I, my dear? I'm sure there must be a spare room somewhere in a house this size. In fact, that's a much better idea. It will allow me more time with Patrick.'

Jordan's short-lived glee promptly evaporated. 'Over my dead body!' he muttered, ushering Virginia inside the house. 'I'm not letting that bitch within spitting distance of my son.'

'You don't seem to have a whole lot of choice,' Virginia pointed out.

'I don't seem to have a whole lot of choice about a number of things,' he said. 'What the hell did you tell her we're engaged for? She obviously doesn't buy it for a minute.'

'I was trying to help you out and it was the first thing that came into my head.' Virginia held out both hands, palms upturned. 'Jordan, that woman means trouble. You've only got to look into those cold green eyes to see that. And why else would she come armed with a court order proclaiming her rights to see Patrick?'

'Don't worry about it, Highness. I know how to handle Marguerite Winslow and her court order.'

'No, you don't,' Virginia said. 'You're so eaten up by dislike for her that you don't begin to see how much she resents you. She *hates* you, Jordan. She's never forgiven you——'

'Yes?'' Jordan gazed at her narrowly. 'Go on, Virginia. What do you know that makes you think I'm in need of Marguerite Winslow's forgiveness?'

Virginia swallowed. Should she tell him that she knew more about his past than he'd ever revealed to her, and that Maria had put her finger on it when she'd said his former in-laws held him responsible for the death of their daughter? That, from the little Virginia had seen in the last fifteen minutes, it was her considered opinion that the Winslows would find ways to punish him for it as long as they both drew breath?

No. This was not the time for lectures or explanations.

'Nothing,' she said. 'Just call it feminine intuition. All I know is, if Mrs Winslow approached me about working for her, I'd run in the opposite direction as fast as I could. I don't trust her.'

'So what are you saying? That I should lie down and let her walk all over me, dishing out orders as if she owns the place?'

'Heaven forbid! I'm just saying that, since she's here whether you like it or not, the whole visit will go a lot more smoothly if she's persuaded that Patrick has settled into a happy and well-adjusted life here, with his father and other grandmother, and...'

'Future stepmother.' Jordan nodded thoughtfully. 'Yeah, I see what you're getting at. Marguerite's a royal pain in the butt but she's nobody's fool and she does love Patrick in her own way.'

'Exactly. So why don't you find him and spruce him up a bit before she sees him, and I'll go and fill your mother in on what's happened.'

'Don't forget to let her know we're engaged,' he said, leering evilly.

'And don't you forget it's a purely temporary arrangement,' she reminded him.

Maria was both horrified and delighted at the unexpected turn of events. 'Engaged!' she sighed, completely ignoring Virginia's explanation that it was an arrangement of expedience only. 'God has answered my prayers! But Marguerite Winslow! Ai, the devil interferes to spoil my happiness! I think I stay in my room for the rest of the afternoon.'

Virginia laughed. 'I'm afraid that won't work. She's determined to stay several days, so we're just going to have to make the best of it,' she said. 'And right now, I need you to come down and help keep her entertained while Jordan gets Patrick ready for inspection.'

But when Jordan joined them downstairs, all he brought with him was the diamond ring. 'I can't find Patrick,' he confided to Virginia in a whisper as they followed Maria outside. 'He's nowhere around. I phoned down to the lodge in case the gates had been left open when the Wicked Witch of the North swooped in—that's all I need, to have her accuse me of letting a five-year-old wander unsupervised all over the countryside. She'd have me in court before the ink's dry on the order—but Thurston assures me he closed them right after she arrived, so that means the kid's got to be somewhere in the garden. I've got the staff out looking for him, so keep your fingers crossed that he shows up in the next five minutes.'

When they trooped outside, Mrs Winslow accepted her Perrier and lime from Maria without so much as a word of thanks and asked in that confrontational way of hers, 'Where is Patrick? I don't see him.'

'But you do see my mother,' Jordan pointed out, 'and I would appreciate your having the courtesy to acknowledge her.'

'Indeed.' The strawberry blonde head tipped briefly in acknowledgement. 'I didn't realize you also were visiting today, Mrs Caine.'

'She's not. She lives here,' Jordan said.

'*All the time*?' came the shocked reply.

'All the time,' Jordan affirmed. 'Patrick, my mother and I, all together under one roof.' He reached out to slide an arm around Virginia's waist. 'And soon to be joined by my beautiful fiancée. Patrick is a very lucky young man, wouldn't you say, Marguerite?'

'That,' Mrs Winslow declared dubiously, 'remains to be seen. What have you got there, Jordan?'

'Virginia's engagement ring. Let's hope it fits.'

It did, perfectly. Even though wearing it was just part of the charade, Virginia couldn't help admiring the diamond's brilliance magnified a thousand times in the sunlight.

'It's quite splendid,' Marguerite conceded, affording it but a cursory inspection as a movement near the marquee captured her attention. 'Ah, *there* he is, my darling little boy!'

As they all turned to watch, Patrick emerged from the tent holding a length of rope, the other end of which was tethered to Tramp's collar. Eyes closed, the child staggered along behind the dog.

'The child is filthy!' Marguerite exclaimed, scandalized. 'And what *is* he doing with that mangy creature?'

'Pretending he's blind,' Virginia said, recognizing at once the game being played.

Ignoring his audience, Patrick continued to follow Tramp's erratic lead, unaware that they were wandering perilously close to the deep end of the pool.

'Patrick, watch out!' Realizing the danger, Jordan sprang forward as he bellowed a warning, but he was a good ten yards or more away from his son and all he succeeded in doing was startle the dog into bolting forward.

In horrible slow motion, Virginia watched as the boy became entangled in the rope, tripped, and did a sort of forward somersault that landed him head first in the water.

Tramp, his makeshift leash dangling beside him, barked agitatedly and ran in aimless circles next to the spot where the child had disappeared.

CHAPTER TEN

MRS WINSLOW screamed and knocked her Perrier all over her Calvin Klein original. Maria gasped and seemed too paralysed with shock to move. But Jordan streaked forward and sliced into the water with such economy of movement that before the three women had time to draw another breath, he had found Patrick and was treading water with his son cradled next to his chest.

'Someone give me a hand,' he yelled.

Grabbing his towel, Virginia raced to help. Between them, they lifted the dazed child to the pool deck. A thin trickle of blood marred his forehead. 'But he's breathing,' Virginia said, her own lungs constricted with a mixture of terror and relief.

'Of course he is,' Jordan said, as if any other option were completely out of the question, but Virginia noticed the pallor beneath his tan. 'He wasn't in the water thirty seconds. He just winded himself when he fell, that's all.'

Maria hurried down to join them. Continuing to scream, Marguerite followed.

'Ai!' Maria lamented, stooping to her knees and pressing Patrick's hands between her own. 'Patrick, *mio bambino!*'

Patrick spat out a mouthful of water, looked up into the ring of anxious faces surrounding him, and burst into noisy tears.

'Everything's OK,' Jordan said, gently probing his son's hairline and exposing a gash perhaps half an inch long.

'Ow!' Patrick's wails intensified. So did Marguerite's screams.

'Will somebody shut that woman up?' Jordan snarled. 'Momma, get me a fresh towel, will you? And tie the dog up before he causes more trouble. Virginia, this cut is going to need stitching and I haven't yet registered with a doctor in the area. Can you recommend someone?'

'Ours,' Virginia said. 'I'll call her right away.'

'Call the ambulance, too, while you're at it,' Marguerite screeched.

'Ambulance?' Jordan snorted, and swung Patrick into his arms. 'Don't be so damned melodramatic, Marguerite! We don't need any ambulance.'

'The boy is bleeding, Jordan!'

'And you're overreacting. Go pour yourself a stiff drink and calm down.'

'I will not! My grandson nearly drowned. This never would have happened if you'd left him with us.'

'Oh, put a sock in it,' Jordan scoffed. 'Patrick tripped and fell. Kids do things like that all the time. If this is the worst that ever happens to him, he'll be damned lucky. And you're missing a few marbles if you think for one minute that I'm about to mollycoddle him the way you did.' He strode toward the house. 'Make that call to your doctor, Virginia, then let's get out of here before I forget what a nice guy I'm supposed to be.'

Dinner that night was not an occasion to which Jordan looked forward with any pleasure, so he prevailed on Virginia to stay and help him entertain his unwelcome guest. 'After all, it's the normal thing for an engaged couple to do,' he argued persuasively, when they returned from the medical clinic. 'In fact, why don't we invite David and Susan to join us, too? Your brother's much better at diplomacy than I am.'

But although that was undeniably true, Virginia refused. 'No,' she said. 'It's bad enough that we're caught up in deceit without involving them, too.'

It was close to seven-thirty before everyone gathered for drinks in the drawing-room. 'Patrick's fine,' Jordan assured the two grandmothers. 'He's got three stitches that will leave him with a temporary hairline scar of which he's very proud. Give him an early night and he'll be none the worse by tomorrow.'

'I, on the other hand, am a wreck,' Marguerite declared, accepting a second glass of champagne. 'That pool is dangerous, Jordan. My poor darling little boy could have drowned.'

'I don't want you talking like that in front of him,' Jordan said testily. 'You'll frighten him off water altogether.'

'I would never deliberately frighten my only grand-child, Jordan. I happen to care very deeply about his welfare.'

'Believe it or not, Marguerite, so do I.'

'Do you?'

'Yes. He is my son.'

'Penelope was your wife. Michele was your daughter. And they are both dead. So you will understand, I'm sure, when I say I find it difficult, if not impossible, to place much faith in your protestations of concern. I think you hold life—*other people's* lives, at least—very cheaply.'

Jordan turned glacial eyes her way. 'I did not invite Virginia here to listen to your grievances on my past per-formance as a husband,' he said, in a low, dangerous voice, 'nor will I tolerate having my mother upset by reminders of a time that caused all of us untold grief.'

'Perhaps Virginia isn't aware of the kind of man you are under those charming good looks, Jordan. Perhaps I'm doing her a favour by letting her know before any wedding takes place. As for your mother...' Marguerite cast a disparaging glance at Maria, who sat in black silk dignity, her expression impassive. 'She is a simple peasant. I doubt she understands the gist of this con-versation in the first place.'

Just then, Mrs Thurston appeared to announce that dinner was about to be served. And not a moment too soon, Virginia thought, heaving a sigh of relief. She'd seen the flush that stained Jordan's cheeks and, even if Mrs Winslow didn't know how narrowly she'd escaped a thorough lambasting for her latest insult, Virginia did.

'Why don't we lead the way?' she asked sweetly, slipping her hand into the crook of Jordan's elbow and nudging him in the ribs at the same time. 'Maria, didn't you tell me earlier that you gave Mrs Douglass your recipe for lamb with garlic and fresh rosemary, and that she was trying it out tonight? I can hardly wait to taste it.'

'Why do I get the feeling you're about to stuff the whole roast in my mouth the minute we sit down?' Jordan muttered through clenched jaws.

Virginia steered him rapidly across the hall to the dining-room, leaving the grandmothers to follow at a more sedate pace. 'Because I might have to do just that if you don't curb your temper,' she muttered back. 'I thought we'd agreed that the only way to deal with someone like Marguerite is to show her you're bigger than she is.'

His blue eyes sparked aggression. 'Behave like the gentleman I'm not, you mean.'

'No, that's not what I mean at all,' she snapped, her own tension flaring in response to his, 'and if, just once, you'd stop treating me as the enemy, you'd realize that. I'm trying to help, Jordan, and heaven knows you need it if this is the best you can do when it comes to dealing with sticky situations!'

'Save the henpecking for someone else, Virginia,' he warned. 'We're not married yet.'

'Nor ever likely to be, in case you've forgotten, but that doesn't mean I don't care what happens to Patrick. Right now, all you're doing is fuelling your mother-in-law's doubts about the sort of father you really are.'

'It's the kind of son-in-law I am that's the real trouble,' he said moodily. 'If I'd just knuckle under and acknowledge that she's never wrong, everything would be peachy.'

'You don't have to go that far. Just don't give her the satisfaction of getting a rise out of you. She's not worth it, Jordan.'

'Relax, Highness,' he said, seating her on the right of his place at the head of the long, polished table. 'I might not have the advantage of your genteel upbringing, but I've got street smarts to make up for it. Where I grew up, people settled their disagreements in a very basic fashion. They spoke their minds and if that didn't work, they used their fists.'

'And wouldn't she just love to goad you into doing that now.'

'You don't have to worry,' he replied sourly, as the other two joined them. 'Even I'm not so unprincipled as to hit a woman.'

Virginia smiled and reached up to kiss his cheek like the devoted fiancée she was supposed to be. It was an easy role to assume. Too easy. 'Of course you're not, my darling,' she murmured theatrically, as much to remind herself of the true state of affairs as to fool Marguerite into swallowing the romantic charade being acted out for her benefit.

For the next forty minutes, everything—the food, the wine, the service and even the conversation—went swimmingly. Voices stayed affable, hackles remained dormant. And then, during a lull between the main course and dessert, Mrs Winslow had to spoil everything.

'Well, this is all very nice, I'm sure, Jordan,' she began, taking stock of the dining-room. 'Very nicely appointed indeed. You're doing much better by your second wife than you did by your first.'

Jordan plastered a smile on his face. 'I have more money now, Marguerite,' he said brazenly. 'Much more.'

'So you will doubtless be able to afford to start another family as soon as you're married?'

Jordan's smile broadened as he glanced at Virginia suddenly cringing with embarrassment. 'I can hardly wait to try, certainly.'

'But what about Patrick? You said yourself, he's only just beginning to adjust to living with you. How will you find the time to devote to him?'

'The same way I do now,' Jordan replied evenly.

Mrs Winslow shuddered delicately. 'Pray heaven you can improve on that!'

Jordan lifted his head and stared at her. 'What's that supposed to mean, Marguerite? That, by your standards, I'm doing a lousy job?'

'I didn't say that,' she replied, rolling her eyes heavenward as though praying for patience. 'I merely meant that although you have acquired money, Jordan, it isn't quite the same thing as having been born to it. Patrick might be enjoying a commendable measure of material comfort and you're certainly playing a more prominent part in his upbringing, but I suspect there's a certain...cultural element missing from his life now.'

'Why?' Jordan asked bluntly. 'Because my mother is a peasant and I'm the son of an immigrant miner, and people like us don't know the difference between painting-by-numbers and real art?'

'Oh, Mrs Caine knows I didn't intend to be offensive when I called her "simple".' Mrs Winslow laughed and made a pretence of reaching across the table to clasp affectionate hands with Maria, who remained unmoved by the overture. '"Simple" is admirable; it's unpretentious. And it in no way detracts from a person's worthiness.'

'As long as that person remembers her place in society and doesn't get ideas beyond her station, right?' Jordan shook his head reprovingly. 'Marguerite, has it never occurred to you that what contributes most to a child's happiness is his knowing that he's loved and well cared for?'

'So well cared for that he practically drowns in an unprotected pool, with his entire family looking on? I find that something of a contradiction.'

'He's lived here several weeks and this is the only time he's come even close to falling in the pool, but if it eases your mind any, I intend to have the area fenced off so that there won't be a repeat performance,' Jordan replied evenly. 'And it wouldn't have happened today if he hadn't been fooling around with the dog and pretending to be blind.'

'Which raises another concern. Why on earth would he resort to such outlandish games?'

'Because he's at that imitative age and Virginia's brother, with whom he spends a lot of time, happens to be blind, that's why. It's just too bad that he decided to show off his acting talents the very same day that my former mother-in-law came trolling up the driveway unannounced.'

'Virginia's brother is blind?'

'Yes,' Virginia said, deeming it a good time to intervene in yet another conversation that threatened to turn into outright warfare. 'Since he was thirteen.'

'Well, that's very tragic, I'm sure, but it hardly inspires my confidence. Between a dog and a blind man, Patrick's hardly receiving the kind of supervision a child his age requires.'

Virginia didn't bother trying to relieve the woman of her ignorance. Not only would it have been a waste of time, she simply wasn't worth the effort. 'Patrick is surrounded by people who love him and want the best for him,' she said, instead. 'Jordan and Maria are devoted to his well-being, and David and I are extremely fond of him. We would never take chances with his safety.'

'A very smooth and—forgive me—very facile reply, Miss Kent, but then, you are not his mother,' Marguerite replied shortly. 'That was Penelope's role. At best, you would be her substitute, and when you have babies of your own you won't want to be bothered with another woman's child.'

'All right, I've heard just about enough!' Jordan sighed with ill-concealed frustration. 'The bottom line,

Marguerite, is that whether or not you like it, I am Patrick's father and I have done nothing to be deemed unfit for the role. He belongs with me. He is happy here.'

'And if he were not? Would you care? Or would your pride get in the way of putting your child's interests ahead of your own?'

'Of course I'd care,' Jordan said wearily. 'I want what's best for Patrick, and that will remain the case no matter how many other children I might have. Stop expecting the worst, for God's sake, and make the most of your visit.'

Somehow, they stumbled through the remainder of the meal, then returned to the drawing-room for coffee. As soon as she decently could, Virginia made her excuses. 'It's been a very long day,' she murmured.

'I'll walk you to your car,' Jordan offered. 'I could use a breath of fresh air.'

'And I'll show Mrs Winslow to her room,' Maria said.

Outside, it was so still that the cry of a loon on the far shore of the lake could be heard although, from the front drive, the water itself was hidden by the bulk of the mansion.

'I hope the weather holds until Saturday,' Virginia said.

'I hope the Wicked Witch has flown south by Saturday,' Jordan replied, taking Virginia's keys and unlocking the door to her car. 'Otherwise, our bogus engagement is going to be made very public and a lot of people will be in for a surprise.'

'Good lord, I hadn't thought about that!' About to slide behind the wheel, Virginia stopped and stared up at him. 'We can't let things go that far, Jordan.'

'We might not have any choice. We've gone to a great deal of trouble to present the picture of a nice happy family and I'm not about to blow the whole thing now. And speaking of surprises, you didn't seem too shocked by what you learned about my past tonight. In fact, you took Marguerite's revelations so well in stride, you might not have been hearing them for the first time.'

'I wasn't,' Virginia admitted. 'Your mother told me about your wife and daughter, the day she came down to our place for tea. That was what we were talking about when you caught us with our heads together.'

He hooked his finger around a strand of her hair and twisted it lightly. 'Why didn't you say so at the time?'

'Because I thought you'd resent having me feel sorry for you. And because I didn't want to get Maria in trouble.'

He pulled her hair a little tighter. 'So why tell me now?'

'Because one lie a day is enough. And because we both know that allowing pity to motivate our actions only complicates things.'

'We're not talking about my marriage now, are we, Virginia? We're talking about our having made love.'

'Yes, and it was a mistake,' she sighed, ducking toward the car, intent only on escaping before she let slip how much she wished things were different between them. 'We have to forget it ever happened, Jordan.'

His arm shot out to bar her way and closed around her. 'But what if I don't want to forget? What if I don't agree it was a mistake?'

'But you do,' she said. 'And the only reason you'd even suggest otherwise is that you think fooling Mrs Winslow into believing we're going to be married strengthens your custodial rights with Patrick.'

'Really? What would it take to convince you you're wrong? This, perhaps?'

His mouth descended on hers, so hot and compelling that hunger shot through her like a flame, threatening destruction of anything standing in its way. What if she were to submit? she found herself wondering. Would it be so terrible?

His lips beguiled, cajoled. One hand caressed her throat and neck, the other threaded itself through her hair with possessive stealth, as if he hadn't already stolen enough of her.

She slipped further under his spell, leaving behind what remained of her sanity. Nothing could be worse than denying a love that persisted in growing despite her most vigorous efforts to stem it, so why didn't she just settle for second-best? It was preferable to nothing, surely, and Jordan needn't ever know how she really felt. One more lie today wasn't going to make that much difference, after all. Was it?

Only for the rest of your life, her heart replied.

'No,' she panted, struggling free of his embrace. 'It takes more than a kiss, Jordan.'

'Still holding out for "I love you" and all that stuff?' he enquired, his voice husky.

'Yes,' she said. 'But I'm not expecting to hear it from you, so don't lose any sleep over it.'

She'd known what his reply would be, but still, when it came, it almost tore her in half. 'Don't worry, I won't,' he said.

Well, that would teach him to lead with his chin!

Scowling, Jordan watched the tail-lights of Virginia's car disappear down the driveway then, itching for a fight, he swung up the steps to the house. For a day that had promised so much, it had certainly deteriorated into total disaster.

He found Maria alone in the drawing-room. 'Has the Wicked Witch gone up to bed already?' he whispered, making a face that had his mother laughing for the first time since Marguerite had blown on to the scene.

'No,' she whispered back. 'As soon as you and Virginia left, she went for a stroll outside to watch the moon rise over the lake, or so she said. I think the truth is that she didn't want to have to make conversation with a peasant. Joey, this engagement between you and Virginia——'

'Is just for show, Momma. I thought Virginia explained that when she talked to you this afternoon.'

'Yes, yes, that is what you both say, but you belong together. I feel it in my bones, in my heart. The two of you fit——' she interlocked the fingers of her right hand with those of her left ' —like this.'

'No, we don't. We come from different worlds and we're poles apart on how we look at things.'

'Love doesn't care about different worlds, my son. It——'

'Momma, please! Asking Virginia to marry me was a mistake to begin with, and she's made it plain that she doesn't consider me suitable husband material, so don't go getting your hopes up that she'll change her mind. You've heard of marriages of convenience? Well, this is an engagement of convenience that will come to an end as soon as we're rid of our guest.'

'She's talking of staying over the weekend,' his mother announced glumly.

Jordan swore under his breath with creative flair. 'I might not always know how things are done in high society, but you taught me to wait to be invited to someone else's house and never to outstay my welcome when I got there. What do you suppose it'll take to dislodge her?'

'She will grow bored very quickly,' Maria said with a shrug. 'There's nothing here to entertain her. You will be at work all day tomorrow, I will be out, and I'm sure she'll find Patrick's company much too noisy. Already she disapproves of the way he behaves.'

Jordan grinned and opened the liquor cabinet. 'You're a wise old cookie, Momma. If he's in his usual form, she'll be out of here by tomorrow night. I'm going to have a brandy. Will you join me?'

Maria shook her head. 'No. As soon as Mrs Winslow comes in and I have shown her her room, I'm going to bed. I have a busy day ahead of me if Virginia's dress is——'

She stopped in mid-sentence. Alerted by her sudden, uncomfortable silence, Jordan looked up sharply.

'Virginia's dress? What have you to do with Virginia's dress, Momma?'

'It is nothing. Just a little arrangement, that is all.'

'What sort of arrangement?'

'Oh, dear.' Hands wringing in dismay, his mother shot him a pleading look. 'Don't be angry, Joey. It is what I wanted and I have been happy doing it.'

'Doing what?' he pursued relentlessly. 'What are you up to that has you stammering and offering explanations that make no sense?'

'I am sewing a dress for Virginia to wear to the Ball,' she confessed miserably.

Jordan glowered at the brandy snifter in his hand and swallowed the caustic words that sprang to his lips. When he felt sufficiently in control of himself, he took a sip of the liquid then turned his attention back to his mother who had sunk into a chair, eyes downcast. 'When did you agree to do this, Momma?' he asked, mildly enough.

She thought for a minute. 'The day I went to tea, I think. No, wait! It was after that. The next day. You had gone away on business and I took Patrick down for his first visit with Tramp.'

In other words, later the same day he'd had the effrontery to propose, Jordan thought bitterly. If this had been Virginia's indirect way of letting him know how far out of line he'd stepped, he must make a point of telling her the message had been received loud and clear. *Kents did not marry the sons of servants.*

'I thought I'd taken you away from all that, Momma,' he said, striving to keep in check the rage that simmered. 'I thought the days were over when you felt you had to work for other people.'

'But it is not work for me,' she cried. 'It is pleasure.'

He looked around at the gracious room, at the fresh flowers on the mantelpiece above the marble fireplace; at the fine mahogany furniture complemented by Oriental rugs and expensive fabrics. He thought of the luxury car parked next to his in the triple garage, and of John Thurston, the driver he'd hired to be at his mother's beck and call twenty-four hours a day; of John's wife who looked after the house, of Mrs Douglass, the cook who took care of the meals. 'And living here like a queen is not?' he asked resentfully.

'Joey, you do not understand.'

'You're right!' he said, his voice rising. 'I don't understand why you'd betray me like this when all I've ever wanted is to make your life better, to give you things you've never had before. What did I forget, Momma, that you'd rather spend your days working at the Kents' house than relaxing here in your own home? What did I do wrong? Tell me and let me put it right.'

'You do not understand,' she said again, her eyes full of a pity he found intolerable. 'It is not how much money a man makes, or how fine his house is, that counts. Those things are nice, but they do not bring happiness.' She made a fist and pressed it to her heart. 'That is something a person finds here, my son. It is knowing you have the freedom to be who you are and not what other people want you to be. It is seeing the goodness in a woman, instead of the wickedness of her father.

'I love you, Joey, and you know I love Patrick. But you are both busy doing the things that make you happy and it is killing me to sit around and do nothing all day. And I am sorry to say that not all your money or position can change the way I feel. A person has to be true to her own heart. So does a man.'

It was the longest speech he'd ever heard his mother make and the passion in it left him feeling ashamed. 'Why didn't you say something before now, Momma?'

She came to him and reached up to hold his face lovingly between her hands. 'Because I know you never meant to be unkind. But if you truly believe I am such a "wise old cookie", listen to me now. Don't let yourself be driven by vengeance and pride. They will eat away your soul and turn your sweetest triumphs sour. You

have come so far, overcome so much. Be brave enough
to go the rest of the way.'

'The rest of the way how?'

'Dare to listen to your heart, my son, before it is too
late.' She pulled his head down and kissed him on both
cheeks. 'Now I go to find Mrs Winslow and tuck her
into bed. I am tired, even if she is not.'

He sat with his brandy for a long time after she'd gone,
restless, dissatisfied, disappointed. Was this to be the
culmination of all his years of effort? A mother who
was unhappy, a mother-in-law so horrified by the job
he was doing as a father that she was questioning his
fitness to raise his son, and a turmoil in his heart that
he couldn't begin to fathom?

He wiped a weary hand across his eyes. Was it really
only this afternoon that he'd been congratulating himself
on a job well done?

Maria finished her sewing by noon on Friday, stayed for
a quick lunch with Virginia, then had Thurston drive her
into Halford to pick up her outfits for Saturday. Virginia
went to see a prospective client, followed that with a
visit to the beauty salon to get her hair trimmed, then
headed back to the mansion where she'd agreed to meet
Maria and help her survive afternoon tea with Mrs
Winslow. As planned, Jordan spent the whole day at the
mine, except for about half an hour around two o'clock
when he apparently came back to the house for some
papers he'd forgotten to take with him in the morning.

All of which probably explained why none of them
realized until nearly four that Patrick was missing. The
last person to have seen him was Mrs Thurston who,
stepping in for Maria, had fed him lunch then put him
down for his afternoon rest.

Initially, no one was unduly alarmed by his disappearance even though a search of the house, pool and
immediate garden area turned up no sign of the child.
'He's just fooling around, hiding somewhere and having

a good laugh at us getting all steamed up over nothing,' Jordan observed.

Marguerite, of course, couldn't resist capitalizing on the situation. 'This is exactly the sort of thing that concerns me,' she said righteously. 'You've made no adequate arrangements for his supervision, which is the main reason the child is running wild and might well be anywhere by now. When he lived with me, I hired a trained nanny to look after him. I would never have dreamed of going out for the morning and leaving him in the care of a housekeeper.'

Mrs Thurston, who'd been dispatched to check Patrick's room, returned in time to hear the comment. 'I was glad to help out. The child is no trouble,' she said, then added cryptically, 'As a rule, that is.'

Jordan looked at her sharply. 'What are you saying, Mrs Thurston?'

She folded her hands over her waist. 'It's not my place to speak out of turn, Mr Caine.'

'I'm inviting your comment. If there's something on your mind, feel free to share it, especially if it has to do with my son.'

'Very well, sir. All things considered, it wouldn't surprise me if Patrick had run away.'

'What on earth makes you think that?'

'He was very upset this morning.'

'About what?'

'About the threat of being taken away from his home and going back to live with his other grandmother.'

'There is no question of that happening,' Jordan assured her firmly.

'The child was led to believe otherwise, Mr Caine.'

A subtle change swept over Jordan. Reserve veiled his features, masking the faint line of worry creasing his brow and leaving his eyes flat and watchful. 'By whom, Mrs Thurston?'

With forthright dignity, she swung her gaze to Marguerite Winslow. It was one of those looks that spoke louder than words.

Marguerite reacted with the aplomb of a woman caught with her fingers in the till. 'Why, that's absurd!' she trilled, her attempt to pass the whole thing off as a joke woefully unconvincing. 'I wouldn't dream of threatening my grandson. I merely mentioned...'

'That you'd spoken to your husband this morning and that wheels had been set in motion. That you'd be leaving soon and taking the boy with you. That nobody in this house really cared about him and that's why they'd all gone off and left him with the only person in the world that truly loved him. That Winslows didn't run wild with mangy, unmanageable dogs and that, once the courts heard what you had to say, they'd hand the child over to you and then it would be off to prep school for him where he'd make suitable friends and relearn his manners in a hurry.' The indictment rolled out of Mrs Thurston's mouth backed by the uncontestable ring of truth.

'Oh, really!' Scarlet fingernails gleaming in the sunlight, Marguerite flapped a disparaging hand. 'As if a five-year-old would be capable of understanding that sort of talk!'

'He understood that you were going to take him away from the people and things he loves. He was upset enough that he could barely get his lunch down and didn't want me to leave him when I put him down for his nap.'

Maria uttered a little wail and sagged into the nearest chair, her face ashen. '*Mio bambino*! It is my fault. I should have taken him with me this morning.'

'No, Momma, it most certainly is not your fault.' Though Jordan's tone was gentle when he spoke to his mother, it changed to biting anger as his erstwhile mother-in-law came under fire again. 'Is it, Marguerite?'

At that, Mrs Winslow's well-preserved face seemed to fold in on itself, losing all its elasticity and leaving little pouches of loose flesh suspended from her jaw. 'Why is everyone staring at me as if I've committed a crime? There's no proof to support either that I'm responsible for Patrick's disappearance or that he's run away.'

'You lied to him,' Jordan said, implacably.

'Don't talk to me about lying,' she flashed back, recovering quickly. 'You're the one pretending to be engaged so that I'll be fooled into believing you're providing a decent, stable family environment for your son when in fact you're conducting a cheap affair practically under his nose. Oh, yes, you might well look taken aback, Jordan, but you forget how noise travels near water. I overheard your conversation with your so-called *fiancée* last night. You condemned yourself out of your own mouth. I have all the proof I need to show that you're no better a father now than you were the day my daughter and her baby ran away from you. The difference is, this time I'm not waiting until a tragedy happens before I do something about it.'

'The tragedy,' Jordan pointed out, his expression forbiddingly remote, 'might already have happened. And if it has, there is no doubt in my mind as to who provoked it. You're never happy unless you're meddling in other people's lives, Marguerite, trying to manipulate and control their every move. Penelope wasn't running away from me, she was running away from——'

Virginia couldn't stand to listen a moment longer. 'Stop it!' she cried, slipping a comforting arm around Maria's heaving shoulders. 'For pity's sake, a child is missing! You disgust me, both of you! If this is any example of your priorities, Jordan, it's no wonder your marriage failed. You and Mrs Winslow are two of a kind, using other people to get what you want. Punishing other people when things go wrong. You deserve each other.'

He turned a frosty gaze her way. 'Thank you for that little homily, Virginia. It makes us all feel so much better.'

She didn't love this man! Virginia thought. She *couldn't* love a man so well-armed against the rest of humanity that nothing touched him except anger and revenge. 'How can you be so cold and unmoved?' she asked, her voice shaking.

'Because getting hysterical won't help matters,' he replied, with a degree of calmness that struck her as downright chilling.

'Then what will?' she whispered. 'How do we go about finding a lost five-year-old? You seem to have all the answers, Jordan, so tell me that. Then, once he's found and safe at home where he belongs and your poor mother's heart has stopped breaking, I promise I won't embarrass you ever again with my uncontrolled hysteria.'

For a long moment he simply looked at her, a strange fire in his blue eyes. Finally, he said heavily, 'Unless anyone has a better idea, I'm going to call the police.'

Mrs Thurston stepped forward again. 'There is one other thing, sir. Patrick's favourite quilt isn't in his room. Wherever he's gone, he's taken it with him. I know, because he had it when I tucked him in for his afternoon nap.'

'The one I made for him, with the red and blue balloons?' Maria quavered. 'Yes, it is his favourite. He always cuddles it when he goes to sleep.'

'Red and blue balloons?' An impression struggled to surface in Virginia's mind. 'I saw something like that just recently.'

'How recently?' For the first time, there was a sense of urgency in Jordan's voice, the faintest inkling that perhaps he wasn't quite as calm as he'd like them all to believe.

She shook her head, trying to sort through the kaleidoscope of thoughts. 'Since we realized he was missing. It was when I...' Slowly, from the jumble of confusion, a picture unscrambled and clarified in her mind's eye: of the jewel-green mark VIII, windows down, parked next to the front door of the mansion; of her cursory glance inside as she passed by. 'When I went to see if he was playing in the driveway. It's on the back seat of your car, Jordan.'

'What?' He stared at her in disbelief. 'Are you sure?'

'It's easy enough to check out,' she said. 'But, yes. I'm sure.'

She was right. The quilt lay draped on the leather seat, half-hidden by rolled-up drawings and a man's light-weight bomber jacket.

'How did it get in here?' Jordan shook his head, puzzled. 'None of this makes any sense.'

Once again, it was Mrs Thurston who supplied the missing pieces. 'I'm afraid it might, sir,' she said, her faded blue eyes worried. 'Ever since you took him to Opal Mountain, the boy's done nothing but go on about it, though why he calls it Old Man Mountain I don't know. But to hear him talk, you'd think it was the most thrilling place on earth instead of a dark old mine——'

'Old Man Mountain, you say? Oh, my God!' Jordan's breath hissed with foreboding. 'You're right, Mrs Thurston. If running away was on his mind, that's where he'd head all right.'

'Don't be ridiculous, man,' Marguerite snapped. 'As I understand it, the mine's a good fifteen miles out of town. How would a child Patrick's age cover the distance without someone spotting him?'

'In the back of a car like this,' Virginia said, craning her neck inside the open window of the coupe to peer on the floor behind the high-backed front seats. 'And unless you made a point of looking, you'd never notice him.' Fear a cold fist clenching at her, she risked a look at Jordan, knowing that his thoughts must be in tandem with her own. 'You were here for just a short time this afternoon,' she said.

His nod was barely perceptible.

'And then you drove——'

'Straight back to the mine. Damn!' Flinging himself into the car, he snatched up the cellular phone resting on the console separating the front seats and rapidly punched in a series of numbers.

Without waiting for permission, Virginia raced around the car and managed to slide into the passenger seat just as he fired the powerful engine to life. She hadn't properly closed her door before he sent the vehicle surging toward the gates.

Things happened quickly after that. A careful driver would have taken twenty-five minutes to negotiate the switch-back road that snaked along the lake shore and up the mountain to the mine. Jordan covered the distance in fourteen minutes flat, saying not a word once he'd finished spitting orders into the phone.

Paul Standwyck, the site manager, was waiting for them as they pulled up outside the big cedar building that housed the general office and miners' facilities.

'Any sign of him?' Jordan asked, bringing the car to a screeching halt.

'You could say that.' Paul handed over a child's navy canvas runner. 'There's no way he could have slipped into the main workings without one of us seeing him, so I ordered a search of the nearby area.' He pointed to a clump of bushes a short way up the hillside. 'You can barely see it from here because of the shrubbery but if you look a bit to the right, there's an old adit up there, probably one of the earliest excavations.'

Jordan accepted the shoe reluctantly and turned it over as though hoping that by some miracle he'd find evidence that it belonged to someone other than his one surviving child. It sat on the palm of his hand, pitifully small and lonely. 'And that's where you found this,' he concluded heavily.

CHAPTER ELEVEN

INTENSELY conscious of the gravity of the situation, Virginia hung back, unwilling to intrude as the two men conferred, but she couldn't help overhearing snatches of the exchange.

'... deserted stope... alluvial... rotting stulls...'

Terminology she'd grown up with came back to haunt her with fearful import. In layman's terms, what they were discussing translated into a tunnel left so long abandoned that it was filling with loose gravel or mud deposited by water seeping through the rock and rotting the timbers erected to support it.

'Jesus!' Jordan wilted against the frame of the mark VIII, dazed with shock and unable to hide it.

Aching for him, Virginia moved closer, stroked a commiserating hand down his arm and twined her fingers around his. There was no answering pressure, no acknowledgement. Indeed, he looked at her almost vacantly, as if she were a complete stranger, before swinging an agonized gaze back to Paul Standwyck. 'We can't just stand here doing nothing. We've got to get a search party inside.'

'That's the whole problem, boss. The area's inaccessible to a grown man——'

'Then we'll have to excavate.'

'No.' Paul shook his head emphatically although regret and compassion etched his features. 'We daren't take the chance, you know that. The inside face is too unstable. You're an expert, Mr Caine. I don't have to tell you the consequences to your boy if we bring on a rock fall.'

'So what do you suggest? That I stand here and blithely put my faith in a God who's never once showed me He gives a damn about me or mine? Or just hope the kid walks out under his own steam? You must be mad!'

'We're investigating a parallel lateral, just in case there's a connecting tunnel.' Paul shrugged helplessly. 'It's the best I can do, boss. There's no one on the payroll small enough to get through that opening the way it stands now.'

'I'll go.' Virginia heard herself make the offer, not because she was brave but because she couldn't bear to think of Patrick, alone and terrified, his every breath a magnified echo in the eerie, utter blackness of the mine. And because Jordan, her darling man of iron, was crumbling inside, racked by a fear he was too proud to own up to and torn by a grief that would never heal if he lost this child, too. She would lay down her life to save him from that.

'No,' he said, his eyes afire in his bleached face. 'I won't allow it.'

Just then, another vehicle drew up. It was the kennel van with Susan at the wheel, David beside her, and a couple of dogs in the back. In addition to Max, his best tracker, David had brought Tramp with him.

'Mrs Caine phoned,' Susan explained. 'We came as soon as we heard. We figured the dogs could help.'

'You think that idiot's going to find my boy?' Jordan eyed Tramp who circled excitedly. 'He couldn't find his own tail in a windstorm.'

'Probably not, which is why Max will do the searching,' David said, gathering the leashes in his hand and laying a soothing hand on the younger dog's head. 'But because Patrick's still a bit nervous of strange dogs, Tramp's the one who'll lure him out, provided someone's there to give him direction.'

Paul shook his head dubiously. 'It's a good idea. The only problem is, the adit's barely wide enough to admit the dogs.'

'If they can get through, so can I.' Virginia planted herself in front of Jordan. 'Let me go, Jordan. Tramp knows me. I can handle him.'

'I already told you, you're not going in.' Jordan swiped a hand across his brow and took refuge in another burst of anger. 'For God's sake, if you can't say something sensible, keep quiet!'

But Paul Standwyck was appraising her body in a way that would have offended her under other circumstances. 'She'll be able to get in, Mr Caine,' he said quietly.

'Absolutely not. I'm not asking her to risk her life.'

'I'm offering anyway,' Virginia said.

Beside her, David rippled with apprehension. 'Virginia ... !'

'What other choice do we have, David? Patrick's just a little boy, probably scared stiff and too disoriented to find his way out again. You and I know how dark and terrifying it is in there, even with an adult present. We both went in as children.'

'No,' Jordan said again.

But she ignored him. 'Tell me what I have to do,' she said to Paul. 'And I hope you've got a helmet in my size.'

He glanced at Jordan, who glowered impressively but remained silent. 'Come with me and let's see what we can find,' he said, leading the way to the main shed.

She might have been in the middle of the earth. Had to keep reminding herself that bright sunlight and open air lay a mere ten feet or so behind her. Had to discipline herself to take even, steady breaths. Had to concentrate on watching where she stepped because, after a brief sniffing of the quilt and shoe, Max picked up Patrick's scent and forged ahead with little regard for the state of her nerves. Already, her sense of direction was completely muddled.

Bent almost double, she clutched the dogs' leashes more firmly and squeezed through a narrow passageway of fallen rock. Without warning, the ground beyond sloped steeply downhill. Barely able to retain her balance, she slithered and slid over loose shale, finally coming to rest at what had once been an old working face of the mine.

Beneath her feet, clammy mud seeped between the straps of her sandals. The lamp on her helmet flung a yellow beak over bulging, dripping walls.

Suddenly, out of the blackness, the skeletal remains of an old support structure swam into view. It marked what she knew was called a level, meaning several connected horizontal openings at that particular elevation. Without Max, she'd have had not the faintest clue which one to take.

'Don't make any more of a disturbance than you have to and move carefully,' Paul had urged, just before she'd shimmied through the narrow, half-buried adit at the surface. 'This section of the mine hasn't been worked in years and we don't know how stable it is. Anything, even an echo, could trigger a fall.'

'That's right,' Jordan had raged in a low, intense voice. 'Go ahead and terrify her. It'll make the day more memorable.'

'She's got to know the risks she's facing, boss,' Paul had said. 'It's only fair.'

'Let Max do the work,' David had urged, and run his fingertips over her face, tracing every feature fondly, anxiously. 'Be careful, Virginia, for all our sakes. Take the time to look around before you go in too deep. He's most likely close to the entrance.'

But the first few feet had been so narrow, there would have been no missing Patrick if all he'd done was hide from the view of the people outside. He'd gone further. Like her, he'd fallen or rolled down the steep incline. And if he'd knocked himself unconscious on the slabs of fallen rock, and was lying face down in the mud, she

might have buried him under the shale she'd disturbed.
Might even be standing on his poor little body and not
even realize it...

Fear disintegrated into outright panic then, battering
her, clutching her. She felt sick, faint. Unable to breathe
in the close musty atmosphere. Her sole instinct was to
get out of that hell-hole. To scrabble and claw her way
back to where the sun poured down and the grass grew
green and sweet. To where Jordan waited, all his hopes
pinned on her.

How would she ever face him?

Horror and hopelessness raged inside her, gripping her
so acutely that she squeezed her eyes shut, as though
doing so would release her from terror's rule.

A sound, frail and uncertain, penetrated her self-
imposed darkness.

Blinking, she looked around and realized that Tramp
was thrashing urgently at her heels, straining to push
past her. Meanwhile, ears erect, tail waving gently, Max
was nosing at a small heap directly in front of them.
And a little boy's pale whimper rose in protest.

Elation made her careless. She burst into tears, the
way any normal woman would when her worst fears
weren't realized. Then she squatted in the slime and muck
left behind by a generation or more of gold miners, and
gathered Patrick in her arms, all the while crooning
reassurances that, truly, Max wasn't going to bite him
and that it was Tramp who was washing his face with
an over-eager tongue.

And she didn't care a bit that, in his excitement, the
young dog was wriggling madly in the confined space
and spattering her with another layer of mud. Until a
shower of gravel from above pebbled faintly on her
helmet and a sort of sigh shivered over the wooden
framework beside her.

And then she remembered Paul's words of caution.
'Don't make any more of a disturbance than you have
to...even an echo could trigger a fall.'

'We have to get out of here,' she whispered, her heart thumping with renewed dread. Scooping the frightened child upright and setting him on his feet, she looped Max's leash around his wrist and hauled Tramp close beside her. 'Quickly, Patrick. Follow the dog. Tramp and I are right behind you.'

Her urgency was contagious. The dogs sensed it and so did Patrick. He pulled back, unwilling to let go of her. Max surged ahead. Tramp whined and pressed his head against her knee.

'I'm scared,' Patrick wailed. 'I want my Papa.'

Oh, me too! Virginia thought, terrified that, unless she could cajole the boy into moving quickly and quietly, they might never make it out alive. More than she'd ever needed anything, at that moment she needed Jordan's strength and his courage, his clear, logical mind and un-wavering refusal to bow to adversity.

Another shower of gravel sprayed down, filming the air with dust. 'Papa's waiting for us outside, sweetie,' she said, fighting to keep the panic from showing in her words. 'We'll both see him in a few minutes. You go first with Max, and I'll follow with Tramp.'

Reluctantly, Patrick obeyed, fighting every inch of the gravelly, slippery slope far more slowly than he must have slithered down. If it hadn't been for Max towing him, he'd never have made it.

They'd covered about half the distance to safety when that eerie sighing began again. This time, though, it didn't die away. It grew and swelled like weary old lungs giving up the ghost. And then it sank into a moan as the old timbers shoring up the level collapsed.

The wall to Virginia's right split in a crack, then bulged menacingly. 'Run!' she screamed, releasing Tramp's leash and shoving Patrick upward with all the force she could muster.

She saw his hand flail out as he fought to find pur-chase on the slippery surface and, by some miracle, grasp a handful of Tramp's fur as the terrified animal surged past him. And then the air was filled with debris again, and gravel was pouring down, and her feet were sliding out from under her, and she was being swept back, down, in a rolling, suffocating, blinding avalanche.

And all she thought was, I should have been brave enough to tell Jordan how much I love him before it was too late.

A small crowd had gathered but nobody said a word. The silence hung like the harbinger of death, stifling, paralysing. Except for her brother and the Susan woman, everyone else stood with gazes glued to the slit in the side of the mountain where she'd disappeared. But Jordan couldn't bear to look. Instead he watched David, who held his head at a bit of an angle, as though listening for something beyond the range of ordinary ears.

What is it? Jordan wanted to ask him. What do you hear?

But the concentration on David's face deterred him. It was as though the man's spirit was reaching down into that foul, dank hell and fortifying Virginia for what she had to endure.

Jordan felt for his watch, flung it a disbelieving glance and rapped sharply against the crystal, refusing to believe so little time had passed since last he'd checked. How far had she gone? What had she found?

A phone rang in the main shed, three muted peals before someone answered. High overhead, a pair of bald eagles circled, their wings black against the deep blue sky. An ambulance swung into the parking area. Who had dared presume they'd need it?

Get the hell away from here, he shouted silently from within his nightmare. We don't need you. We *won't* need you! Go find someone else to save.

The paramedics paid no attention. Instead, they opened the ambulance's rear double doors and rolled out two wheeled stretchers.

A sound at his side diverted him. It was her brother inhaling sharply. 'What's the matter?' Jordan demanded, grasping the man's elbow.

And then he heard it, too, the low, murderous underground rumble that turned every miners' blood to ice. Heart thudding, he switched his gaze to the adit and saw the tell-tale puff of dust fly out.

A collective gasp issued from the crowd. Swatting aside the men blocking his way, Jordan charged forward, prepared to wrestle the bloody mountain apart with his bare hands if he had to. It had robbed him once. It wasn't getting away with it again. It wouldn't take his boy. It wouldn't take her. It wouldn't crush and mutilate her lovely body or smother her laughter or silence her voice.

Then, in a different, exultant tone, someone in the crowd exclaimed, 'My God!' and a cheer went up.

He stopped in mid-stride, looked again at the place where she'd disappeared, and did something he'd never before done in public. He allowed the tears to roll down his face. Because, in the wake of that calamitous puff of dust, the tracking dog came surging through the adit, Tramp racing beside him, and last, tagging along at the end of the leashes like a stray piece of laundry on a washing line, Patrick.

The paramedics ran forward, metal first-aid kits swinging from their hands, but Jordan hung back, poised like a runner waiting for the crack of a starting gun. One second passed, and then another, before he realized that the shout of elation had dribbled away, aborted by an uneasy hush.

This time it was her brother who couldn't bear the silence. 'What is it?' he demanded, groping for his ladyfriend's arm. 'Susan, what do you see?'

Jordan stared at the sun-flecked clump of shrubbery. Blinked to relieve the stress and anxiety of the last two hours that had left his eyeballs feeling as if they were rolling in grit, and stared again at the blank and arid hillside.

Around him, murmurs of shock and disappointment confirmed what he was trying to avoid having to accept: that Patrick and the two dogs were tumbling down the slope, grimy but unharmed. And after them . . . nothing.

The rising hum of consternation galvanised him. A surge of adrenalin roared through him. Louder than all the rest, a voice that he knew to be his damned creation.

He felt hands trying to hold him back. Saw dismay turn to pity on the faces of those around him. Wanted to bellow with rage at the inaction of the bystanders when every second counted.

'Jordan, no!' Standwyck begged, hanging on to the sleeve of his shirt with the determination of a terrier. 'We don't know how bad things are down there. Let one of us go instead.'

With a vicious jerk, he flung the man off and sent him rolling back down the hill. 'Try to stop me,' he snarled, 'and I'll tear you in half.'

Leaving them all in the dust of his rage, he squeezed himself through the adit, clawing and cursing every miserable inch of the way. 'All right, Old Man,' he panted, plummeting into a dark well of dirt and gravel and feeling the mountain close around him, 'if it's a fight you want, you've got it. But I'm going to win. This is one treasure you're not keeping for yourself.'

The mountain responded with all the vicious brutality of which it was capable, propelling him in a verticle nosedive down a chute lined with fine rock that pumiced his forearms and ribs. He ended in a dazed heap at the bottom, in a cave formed by the fallen cross-sections of an old stull.

It took him a moment to realize that the reason he could see all this was that the scene was illuminated in a ray of light beaming at a drunken angle from the top of a miner's helmet. And below it, its natural pale gold dulled by grime, spilled a mass of wavy hair.

Squirming until he was hunched on his hands and knees, he crawled forward. 'Virginia?' he croaked, his mouth and throat so thick with dust he could barely articulate.

Her whisper floated back to him, tentative as a new-born's first breath. 'Jordan?'

So swamped with relief that he couldn't bear it, he did what he always seemed to do when she threatened his heart too violently. He took refuge in anger. 'What the hell are you doing here?'

He didn't give a rap that, battered on all sides by spiteful little pebbles as she'd been tumbled down that slope, her whole life had flashed before her eyes. Or that she was fighting to hang on to her senses because she thought she might faint and, if she did, she was afraid she might never wake up again.

He didn't give a rap that she could just as well have been dead. In fact, she thought blurrily, finding a corpse might have been more to his liking. Obviously, discovering her, alive and relatively unharmed, did not strike him as cause for celebration.

'Collecting ideas for a new style of décor,' she mumbled, the ghost of her usual spark struggling to ward off the encroaching darkness. 'What's your excuse?'

'What does it look like? Effecting a heroic rescue, of course.'

A different kind of fear assaulted her. 'You mean Patrick and the dogs didn't...make it?'

'Of course they did,' he snapped. 'I'm here to get you out, you daft woman. Or did you think I'd order the adit sealed with you still inside, and leave your bones to rot in peace?'

She formed her reply with great care because relief left her so light-headed that her mouth felt as if it were full of cotton wool that kept getting wrapped around her tongue. 'It...wouldn't surprise me a bit, knowing how you...feel about me...'

'Fat chance!' He tossed his head derisively and in doing so spattered her with a shower of fine grit that flew out of his hair. 'You're tiresome enough that your ghost would probably haunt me the rest of my days.'

She started to laugh then—at least, that was what she thought she was doing—but the sound that came out was oddly high-pitched, like a mouse caught in a fit of squeaking giggles. Embarrassed, she covered her mouth with her hand and felt the terror and stress of this last small lifetime seep out of her eyes in a slow-rolling spate of tears. Jordan must be *so* annoyed!

'Oh, hell,' he muttered, crawling closer.

She took a deep breath and tried to tell him to leave her alone, that she didn't want or need his help. That she'd managed to get in by herself and she'd manage to get out the same way. But the sides of the tunnel were beckoning her, the left side merging with the right in rippling, slow-motion waves that numbed her brain.

'Don't you dare pass out on me,' Jordan threatened from a great distance. 'Not until you've hauled your pretty little backside back up that chute.'

The mere thought of attempting such a feat was the last straw. With a sigh, she defied him and gave in to the stifling, fuzzy darkness. It was much kinder than the light...

She went on a long journey over rough terrain. Jiggled and joggled like a sack of potatoes on the back of a donkey. Climbed a mountain so steep that her arms felt as if they'd pull right out of their sockets. But it was worth it because when she got to the top, it was beautiful. Full of the scent of wild poppies and fresh air and cool water. And so soft that she stopped hurting and could pay attention to the voice.

Such a lovely voice it was. Deep and tender, even though it bullied her unmercifully. But it didn't frighten her. Wherever she was, she knew she was safe. It would be all right to rest and let the bad dream melt away...

*   *   *

She woke to a different voice. Melodious, familiar, maternal. And gentle hands stroking her cheek. 'There now, *cara*, that's it. Open your eyes.'

She was in a room full of delicate purple shadows. A room she'd seen before, with filmy white draperies billowing in the soft air of evening. She lay on a bed as high as a barge, pillowed in downy white comfort. A face swam into view, round and smiling, with silver hair pulled back in a chignon.

'Is she coming to, Momma?' It came from the shadows, that lovely masculine rumble she'd heard in her dream, not browbeating now, but full of uncertainty.

'Yes. Come and talk to her, Joey.'

The gentle hands and face withdrew, leaving her momentarily afraid. 'Maria?' she whimpered, as memory returned in graphic, horrific detail. What a pathetic creature!

'I am here, *cara*.'

'We both are, Virginia.'

He loomed over her, the only man she'd ever love. His blue eyes mesmerised her, banished the fear and drew her out of the dark more potently than any medicine. By some miracle she was safe. She was going to live. She was not condemned to die, a little at a time, at the bottom of a derelict mine tunnel.

She felt life stirring within her, felt her lips turn up in a little smile. 'What the hell are you doing here, Jordan?' she asked, in a near-normal voice.

He didn't smile back. Instead, he lifted her hands and kissed her palms, then buried his face against them. His broad, beautiful shoulders trembled.

'Don't cry,' she said softly.

His head shot up. He sniffed and glared and thrust out his jaw belligerently. 'As if I would!' he snorted. But his eyes, she noticed, were glassy with unshed tears.

She cupped his face and looked at him. At first, he refused to meet her gaze, then suddenly changed his mind and sank his cheek next to hers. 'If you only knew how I felt, knowing you were trapped...' he began.

She sensed that there were things he wanted to tell her, if only he could find the words. That, as a result of that day's events, he'd reached certain conclusions regarding him and her. Although she tried to dampen it, a surge of optimism possessed her. 'Tell me,' she urged. 'How did you feel, Jordan?'

If she'd hoped—and she had!—that asking him a leading question would prompt him to cast aside all reservation and tell her he loved her, he promptly taught her the folly of succumbing to such rubbish. 'Scared half to death,' he mumbled. 'We thought we'd lost you, Virginia.'

We, he said, not *I*. Was that deliberate? She had to find out. 'Would it have mattered so very much if you had?'

He reared away from her touch as though she were infected with something catching. 'Woman,' he warned, backing toward the door, 'don't push your luck! You've done enough for one day and I'm in no shape to deal with any more of it.'

'You're the one who brought the subject up to start with. All I'm——'

He shook his head. 'Not now,' he ordered. 'I know there are things that need to be said, but for Pete's sake, not now. I'm all frayed around the edges and not thinking clearly. Anyway, there are people waiting for me downstairs. Reporters and such, wanting a story, you know?'

No, she felt like retorting. I don't know. If you can talk to them, why not to me?

But behind him, the door opened to admit Maria. 'Thank God you've come back,' he muttered and, seizing his chance, fled the scene.

Laughing, Maria came over to Virginia and set a bowl of pale green grapes on the table beside her. 'Already

the roses are coming back to your cheeks, *cara*. You are
feeling better and so, I see, is my son.'

'Yes,' Virginia agreed glumly. 'How did I get to be
here, Maria?'

'You know where you are, then?'

'Of course. In Jordan's bedroom. But why not in
mine, in my own house?' Where *everyone* would be glad
to see her making such a swift recovery and no one would
dream of suggesting she was pushing her luck!

'He would not hear of it,' Maria said, with a shrug.
'Refused to have you out of his sight for a moment.
When the ambulance men said they should take you to
the hospital, my son, my wicked Joey, used so many bad
words that I must spend the next week apologizing to
all who heard him. ''She will come to my house where
she belongs, and I will call her doctor,'' he said. ''You
don't give the orders here, I do.'''

As if anyone of sound mind could ever suppose
otherwise! 'I've heard enough about Jordan, Maria.
How's Patrick?'

'Oh, Patrick is full of admiration for himself.' Maria's
dark eyes danced. 'The brave child, he saved Signor
David's dogs, did you know that?'

Belatedly, Virginia realized that her obsession with
trying to worm a loving word out of Jordan had allowed
her no time to consider how her brother or Susan were
coping. They must be frantic with worry.

She flung aside the bed covers. 'I have to get home
right away and let my family know that I'm all right.'

Maria slapped the duvet back in place. 'No, *cara*. You
are to stay here until tomorrow. You've had a bad shock
and must have a quiet night. Joey insists.'

Joey be damned! 'That's ridiculous! I have a perfectly
good bed of my own at home and David will be expecting me. Where are my dress and shoes, Maria?'

'The dress is being laundered, but the shoes . . .' Maria
rolled her eyes significantly. 'Virginia, those shoes are
past saving. I am afraid they have been thrown away.

But your friend Susan was thoughtful. When she came over, she brought you a bag with some clean clothes and a few other things that she thought you might need.'

'Susan is here?'

'Didn't Joey tell you? She and your brother are both downstairs. They and those wonderful dogs are the guests of honour at dinner tonight.'

'Then I shall join them and later we can all go home together.'

'I think not, *cara*.' Maria bustled over to the windows and drew back the drapes. Across the lake, the sun was going down in a classic blaze of glory. 'You may bathe and change into something more comfortable, but then you must come back to bed and I will bring you a light supper.'

'On whose orders?' Mutinously, Virginia tossed off the duvet a second time and swung her legs to the floor. But to her amazement, her knees almost buckled beneath her. 'Good grief,' she murmured, clutching at Maria, 'I feel weak as a kitten.'

'Exactly. The doctor told us it would be so.' Maria nodded emphatically and slipped an arm around her waist. 'You had a bad shock, *cara*, but you are young and strong. A bath and a good night's sleep will work wonders. Do as you're told tonight and, by tomorrow at this time, you will dance and be the belle of the Miners' Ball.'

Relaxing in the opulent decadence of Jordan's private bathroom, Virginia was inclined to believe Maria might be right. With humming, hypnotic frenzy, the whirlpool tub pummelled her aches into submission and filled her with pleasant lassitude. The hot water scoured away every trace of grime, the thick velvet towels massaged her dry as tenderly as if she were a baby.

She pulled on a blue cotton nightshirt she discovered in the bag Susan had brought, brushed her hair and teeth, and found the prospect of crawling no further than the bed in the next room infinitely more appealing than trying to smuggle herself into the back of the van and sneaking home.

When Virginia returned to the room, Maria had gone down to dinner but Mrs Thurston had taken her place and was turning down fresh sheets on the bed. 'You've got a visitor waiting outside,' she said. 'Shall I send him in when you're settled?'

Anticipation that it was Jordan caused a flutter that sent her heart staggering. 'Yes, please.'

But, guided by Susan, it was David who came through the door. 'How are you feeling?' he asked, folding Virginia's hands in his.

'Better by the minute,' she assured him, 'which is more than I can say for either of you. You look terrible.'

'Gee, thanks!' David's laugh wasn't quite as free as usual. 'You would, too, in the same circumstances.'

'It was hard on all of us but particularly for David,' Susan said, hugging her. 'He was virtually stranded in the middle of utter pandemonium and no one could tell him exactly what was happening because no one really knew. First, you disappeared inside the mine and didn't come out again, then Jordan went charging in after you like a raging bull, despite everyone else's attempts to stop him. There wasn't much the rest of us could do but wait and hope for the best.'

'The miners who'd formed the initial search party were afraid he'd cause another fall and they'd never get either of you out alive,' David put in. 'I can tell you, Virginia, there aren't too many times when I bother wasting energy railing over the fact that I can't see, but this afternoon was one of them. Then, when I heard them talking about lowering a sling to get you back to the surface...'

He stopped and drew a shaky breath. Susan squeezed his shoulder then slid her hand up and massaged the back of his neck with what struck Virginia as something more intimate than mere sister-like concern.

Trying not to look overly intrigued, she asked, 'Why did they need a sling?'

'Because,' Susan explained, massaging away, 'they heard Jordan bellowing up the tunnel that it was too steep and narrow and the gravel underfoot too unstable for him to be able to carry you out himself. Luckily, the worst of the fall occurred further in, past the place where he found you, and you probably wouldn't have needed rescuing at all if you hadn't fainted.'

His composure restored, David leaned into Susan's tender ministrations and grinned. 'Susan told me it was like a scene from a movie when Jordan came striding down the hillside with you in his arms. Too bad you slept through the romantic drama of the moment, Sis!'

'I'm just as glad I did. I must have looked a mess.'

'You weren't at your pristine best,' Susan agreed. 'Speaking of which, I thought you'd appreciate a change of clothes so I hope you don't mind my rummaging through your drawers.'

Virginia fingered the fabric of the nightshirt so soft against her skin. 'Not a bit. It's not the most glamorous outfit, but it's clean and comfortable and believe me, after this afternoon, those are two things I'll never take for granted again.'

Her visitors left soon after and Virginia found herself confronting a truth she hadn't foreseen. David and Susan were in love and probably had been for months! How could she have been so wrapped up in her own confused liaison with Jordan that she'd failed to notice another romance blooming right under her nose?

She sighed and closed her eyes to hold back a sudden spurt of tears. Not because she was resentful that another woman had supplanted her in her brother's life; she truly wanted only the best for David, which was exactly what he'd be getting in Susan. It was more that Virginia felt just a bit empty because David and Susan had found the kind of happiness in each other that she had hoped might be hers to find with Jordan.

But for all that he'd left her with the impression that there were things left unsaid between them, Jordan had taken the first chance to escape that presented itself and didn't seem in much of a hurry to put in another appearance and pick up where he'd left off.

She was half inclined to believe that rare moment of emotion he'd shown had been a figment of her imagination. That, or the after-effects of shock that left her weak and weepy had restored him to his usual pragmatic self, the one that never allowed him to betray a moment's weakness.

Oh, what was the use of wishing for something he didn't have to give? she thought dispiritedly. Love either happened or it didn't. In his case, it didn't.

CHAPTER TWELVE

HE CAME to her when all the dinner guests had gone home and everyone else was sleeping. She had been lying wide awake, lamenting the fact that it was a night drenched in the scent of roses and thick with stars—midsummer enchantment waiting to happen, but with no one in the wings to set it in motion—when the door clicked softly open and Jordan slipped through quietly as a shadow.

'Virginia?' he whispered. 'Are you awake?'

Just briefly, Virginia considered giving a loud, unladylike snore, to teach him a lesson for keeping her waiting so long, but she was past playing games. 'Yes,' she said. 'I thought you'd changed your mind.'

He loped silently across the thick white rug and perched on the side of the bed. 'I tried to,' he confessed. 'I just didn't have the stamina to follow through on it.'

She rose up on one elbow, giddy with sudden hope. 'I'm so glad. It saves me the indignity of having to come looking for you. Because, whether or not you have anything more to say to me, Jordan, there is something I must tell you.'

'You're going to make me confront the truth, aren't you?' he asked morosely.

'Yes.'

He groaned. 'You're going to make me walk through fire and wear a hair shirt.'

'No,' she said. 'That might come with confronting *your* truth but I'm talking about mine.' She stopped and drew a deep breath to fortify her courage. 'I thought I might die this afternoon, Jordan, and I realized that, if I did, my biggest regret would be that I didn't tell you I loved you when I had the chance.'

There, it was out! What happened next was up to him. He might laugh or sneer, and if he did she'd have to learn to live with it because anything was better than not knowing how he felt about her.

He did neither, and instead spent rather a long time just looking at her. Then he said, 'You know, of course, that according to Marguerite, I'm a monstrous, miserable son-of-a-bitch whose track record with women stinks?'

'Yes.'

'And that I don't suffer fools gladly.'

'I'm no fool,' she said.

'Perhaps not,' he said, taking a different tack, 'but has it occurred to you that the reason you think you...er, feel this way about me——?'

'The word is "love", Jordan, and saying it out loud won't make the world come to an end. And I don't "think" I love you, I *know*.'

'Yes, well . . .' He cleared his throat. 'Could it be that you've talked yourself into believing that because I'm the one who robbed you of your virginity?'

'You didn't rob me,' she corrected him. 'I gave it to you freely.'

'Sex isn't the same thing as love, Virginia.'

'No, it isn't. From the little I know about it, sex is beautiful and breathtaking but its impact fades rather quickly. Unlike love, which endures despite a person's best efforts to ignore it.'

He sighed and looked toward the window. Projecting a serenity she was far from feeling, she followed his gaze. What she really wanted was to touch him, but she was afraid he might back away from her if she made the slightest move.

She wished with all her heart that he would reach out to her. He didn't have to go so far as to meet her halfway; she simply wanted him to make some gesture, however small, to show that he wasn't rebuffing her. But he didn't and so, for a nerve-racking space of time, they sat as still as statues while the moon sailed high over the lake and rippled the water with silver.

At last he turned to look at her again. 'The reason Penelope and I got married,' he said, 'had less to do with love than it had with what we could do for each other. She gave me a foot up the social ladder by introducing me to the élite, and I protected her from her dragon of a mother and overbearing father. We covered our weaknesses with all the outward trappings of a smart, successful young couple, and thought that would be enough. But it wasn't. We were so busy protecting our personal insecurities that we had nothing left over with which to nurture our marriage.'

He sighed again, the way a person might before he jumped from a sinking ship and consigned himself to the mercy of a man-eating shark. 'But you won't let me get away with that, Virginia. You make me confront my worst fears and self-doubts. You make me aware of those things lacking in my life that money and position have never been able to buy. You make me acknowledge that there are some things over which a man has no control. And I decided, a long time ago, that I would never relinquish control of my life to anyone, ever again.'

'Are you saying that there's no future for you and me?' Again, by the grace of a truly merciful God, she managed to sound composed, even though she knew, if it was escape he was seeking, her question had opened the door for him.

'What I'm telling you,' he replied irascibly, 'is that I'm bloody well in love with you and prepared to crawl over hot coals, if that's what it takes to prove it. The day I went out and bought that ring was the day I sold my soul—to you. I just wasn't prepared to admit it at the time. You gave me all the trappings when you redecorated this house, Highness, but it isn't enough. *You* are what makes it a home. It's incomplete without you—a setting without a play, a love story without a heroine.'

She'd never thought to hear such poetry falling from Jordan Caine's lips. Was she dreaming? 'Why, Jordan,' she breathed, a flood of joy billowing inside her, 'do you mean to say that when you asked me to marry you, you really meant it?'

'Hell, yes! I'm not fool enough to toss around marriage proposals unless I'm prepared to have them taken seriously.'

'Is it too late for me to change my mind about accepting?'

'No,' he said. 'But before you agree to anything you might live to regret, think about what you'll be taking on. I come encumbered with a son and a mother, both of whom need me. Perhaps I deserved to have my first marriage fail, but I do not intend to put myself or my family through the trauma of another break-up. So take a long, hard look at what you'll be getting, Virginia, because there's no refund or exchanges on this deal.'

'Why would I want either,' she whispered, at last daring to lean forward and slip her arms around his neck, 'when I'll be getting the best?'

He let out a long, slow breath then pulled her close and inched his mouth to hers with purposeful stealth. Briefly, sweetly, before the passion took hold, he pledged himself to her with a kiss that was infinitely tender. 'I will love you,' he promised hoarsely, 'for the rest of my life.'

She savoured that kiss and stored it in her heart as a talisman against those rocky passages that she knew were part and parcel of every marriage. But then his lips grew bolder, straying from her mouth to her throat, and from there to her shoulder, setting off a deep, exultant throbbing within her as relentless as a jungle tom-tom.

She pressed a hand to the back of his head, holding him captive at her breast as the blind, imperative hunger threatened to swamp her. 'Aah, Jordan ... !' Caught between a sigh and a moan, his name slipped loose.

He pushed her back against the pillows. Followed after and pinned her beneath him. 'Stop squirming like that, my darling,' he commanded unsteadily, 'or making love to you will be over before either of us has time to enjoy it.'

Propriety made a feeble effort to assert itself. She was, after all, a guest in his home, as was his former mother-in-law whose room was just down the hall. 'Shh!' she whispered. 'What if someone—Marguerite—should hear?'

He pulled her nightshirt over her head and shucked off his own clothes with astonishing speed. 'Marguerite left this evening and won't be back for a while,' he replied, his hand at her hips persuading them into closer affinity with his. He traced a line from her throat to her navel with a vibrantly gentle forefinger. 'Have I told you before that I think you're beautiful?'

'No,' she said.

He dropped a kiss on her shoulder, another on the inside of her wrist. 'You are exquisite, inside and out; so full of light and lovelinesss that I will never understand how it is that some other man hasn't claimed you before now.'

'I was waiting for you,' she told him, feasting her eyes on the fine, male magnificence of him.

'Then I must make sure I don't disappoint you,' he said.

Her first instinct, to freeze with shock, melted in the rush of delirium that swept over her. Wave after wave, it assaulted her like nothing she'd ever known before, rippling from the soles of her feet to the roots of her hair.

Desire a liquid ache she could not repress, she heard herself begging him to come to her, to fill the aching void he'd created within her. Felt herself reaching for him, closing around him, guiding, urging.

He followed willingly, forging a bond between them that, under his direction, ebbed and flowed with awesome, rhythmic power. He whispered in her ear, sweet nothings that she would cherish to her dying day. He called her 'darling' and 'sweetheart' and told her there had never been a woman like her; never would be, ever again. She had not known it was possible to feel so safe or so well loved.

Then, slowly, irrevocably, control slipped away, no longer his to command. Beneath her hands, the muscles of his shoulders tensed. His hips stilled. His thighs locked on either side of hers, immobilising her. The little words of love faded away into strained silence. He lowered his forehead to hers and inhaled deeply and carefully.

It didn't do any good. There was no stopping, no way to retrace the course. The cadence picked up again, exquisite and rather terrifying. Altered, deepened to a heavy roar. Became a swelling torrent that snatched them up and tossed them heedlessly about until it tired of its game and outpaced even itself. And then, with malicious mischief, tossed them over the rapids and into oblivion.

Virginia expected never to surface. Feared she'd never breathe again. Thought the drumming of her heart had left her permanently deafened. Could scarcely muster the energy to unclench her hands from their death grip on his hair, and failed to understand how her legs would ever regain the strength to support her. Surely she was condemned to spend the rest of her life in the vacuum left behind by such a surfeit of agonized pleasure?

Not so. Gradually, the night reclaimed her, filtering quietly into her consciousness. The faint echo of music floated from somewhere across the lake. The filmy draperies puffed out on a sigh of wind.

Jordan lifted his head and, in the diffused light from the moon, she saw him smile down at her. And that was when she knew, for sure, for certain, that it hadn't been a dream. It was real, every earth-shaking, wonderful minute of it.

'I wish you didn't have to leave me tonight,' she said.

'I don't,' he said. 'I'll never leave you ever again.'

She had thought she'd learned all the best there was
to know about loving, but she was wrong. The avid, de-
vouring hunger, he showed her, bending his head to her
once again, could soften to drowsy, languorous pleasure.
'We have all night,' his mouth and hands told her. 'We
have the rest of our lives.'

It was the hour between sunset and moonrise; a magic
time of indigo hills against an apricot sky. Chinese lanterns strung through the trees illuminated couples
strolling in the gardens. The brass and percussion of big
band dance music filtered through the graceful arched
windows of the ballroom to blend amiably with the jazz
combo pounding out its rhythm in the striped marquee.
Champagne flowed, jewels glittered.

If the measure of a man's stature was gauged by others'
perception of his success, today he had achieved the ultimate triumph. From the afternoon reception and buffet
to the formal events of the evening, Opal Lake society
had turned out in record numbers to pay tribute to
Jordan Caine and welcome him to its top-drawer ranks
with open arms.

Strange how things worked out sometimes, he thought.
Six months ago, he'd have said he could want for nothing
more. Tonight, he knew he could walk away from it all
without a single regret because none of it amounted to
a hill of beans on the real scale of things. What mattered
was that he had his family, and he had Virginia. And
for the first time in his life, that was enough.

He turned back into the room, his gaze, squinting
against the dazzle of the chandeliers, roaming the perimeter of the dance floor until it found her. Her dress,
dark blue and shimmering with beads, made her skin
glow like warm ivory. She wore her hair piled on her
head in a pale topknot of curls. He had never seen her
look more beautiful.

Glancing up, she caught his gaze and waited for him,
tranquil as a dove and so thoroughly at ease that some-

thing of her serenity communicated itself to his mother
who stood beside her with hands calmly folded and a
small, interested smile on her face.

'No one would guess you were shaking with nerves an
hour ago, Momma,' he teased, coming up to them. 'You
look every inch the *châtelaine*.'

'That is a job for a wife,' his mother informed him,
casting a sly glance at his arm as he slid it around
Virginia's waist.

'Perhaps you're right,' he said. 'Will you be OK by
yourself for a few minutes? I have a little unfinished
business to take care of with Virginia.'

He took her outside, to a quiet corner of the flagstone
terrace. There, screened from view by a potted bou-
gainvillaea, he pulled her close and kissed her so
thoroughly that she clutched at the silk lapels of his
jacket to keep herself upright.

'I've been itching to do that all evening,' he said. 'How
much longer do you suppose people are going to stay?'

'Jordan!' she laughed. 'It's only nine o'clock. They'll
be here for hours yet.'

'Will they miss us if we sneak away?'

'Yes,' she said. 'You're the host—and the star. You've
worked a miracle and put this town back on its feet, and
people want to let you know how proud and grateful
they are.'

'You did a wonderful job organizing everything,
Highness,' he said, his voice and eyes caressing her. 'Blue
collar and white both appear to be having a good time.'

She linked her arms around his neck. 'Happiness is a
great equalizer.'

'It might take me a while to get used to that. Happiness isn't something I've had a lot of experience with
in recent years.'

'Is there anything I can do to make the
transition easier?'

'Yes,' he said, lifting a small, tissue-wrapped object from his breast pocket. 'You can accept this when I offer it to you a second time. Then you can stand beside me while I tell all those people in there that you've just agreed to be my wife, and maybe then they'll get the message and cut the evening short. Well?'

The perfect diamond flashed blue fire into the night. 'Yes,' she said.

'Yes? Just like that, with no argument?'

'Yes.'

He grew very still, as if he thought that, by moving too suddenly, the happiness he'd found might take fright and disappear. When he trusted himself to speak again, his voice was husky with emotion and his long black lashes swept down to hide whatever might be revealed in his blue eyes. 'You have just made my mother a very happy woman,' he said, sliding the ring on her finger. 'Don't you think, my darling, that it's time we let her know?'

'Not until I tell you again how much I love you,' Virginia whispered.

'And how much is that?' he muttered, almost choking on the question.

She reached out a fingertip and touched it to the one foolhardy tear that had dared to slip free and roll down his cheek. When he tried to turn away so that she couldn't see, she cupped his face and forced him to look at her. 'How much?' she echoed tenderly. 'There are no words to tell you. Better I should try to count the stars.'

But if words failed her, action didn't. And so she showed him instead.

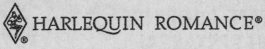

HARLEQUIN ROMANCE®

brings you:

A letter has played an important role in all our romances in our Sealed with a Kiss series so far, and next month's WANTED: WIFE AND MOTHER by Barbara McMahon is no exception.

But for Caroline Evans, the letter from Australian rancher Nick Silverman comes as something of a shock. His letter isn't sealed with a kiss—it's a coldhearted proposal! Nick needs a mother to take care of his little orphaned niece, Amanda. And Caroline needs to marry to fulfill the conditions of her great-aunt's will. A marriage of convenience seems an ideal solution for all three of them but, with a cynical and sexy stranger for a husband, has Caroline taken on more than she can handle?

Don't miss Harlequin Romance #3369
Wanted: Wife and Mother by Barbara McMahon

Available in July wherever Harlequin books are sold.

SWAK-5

ANNOUNCING THE

PRIZE SURPRISE SWEEPSTAKES!

This month's prize:

L-A-R-G-E—SCREEN PANASONIC TV!

This month, as a special surprise, we're giving away a fabulous FREE TV!

Imagine how delighted you and your family will be to own this brand-new 31" Panasonic** television! It comes with all the latest high-tech features, like a SuperFlat picture tube for a clear, crisp picture...unified remote control...closed-caption decoder...clock and sleep timer, and much more!

The facing page contains two Entry Coupons (as does every book you received this shipment). Complete and return *all* the entry coupons; **the more times you enter, the better your chances of winning the TV!**

Then keep your fingers crossed, because you'll find out by July 15, 1995 if you're the winner!

Remember: The more times you enter, the better your chances of winning!*

*NO PURCHASE OR OBLIGATION TO CONTINUE BEING A SUBSCRIBER NECESSARY TO ENTER. SEE THE REVERSE SIDE OF ANY ENTRY COUPON FOR ALTERNATE MEANS OF ENTRY.

**THE PROPRIETORS OF THE TRADEMARK ARE NOT ASSOCIATED WITH THIS PROMOTION.

PTV KAL

PRIZE SURPRISE
SWEEPSTAKES
OFFICIAL ENTRY COUPON

This entry must be received by: JUNE 30, 1995
This month's winner will be notified by: JULY 15, 1995

YES, I want to win the Panasonic 31" TV! Please enter me in the drawing and let me know if I've won!

Name_____

Address _____ Apt. _____

City   State/Prov.   Zip/Postal Code

Account #_____

Return entry with invoice in reply envelope.

© 1995 HARLEQUIN ENTERPRISES LTD.   CTV KAL

PRIZE SURPRISE
SWEEPSTAKES
OFFICIAL ENTRY COUPON

This entry must be received by: JUNE 30, 1995
This month's winner will be notified by: JULY 15, 1995

YES, I want to win the Panasonic 31" TV! Please enter me in the drawing and let me know if I've won!

Name_____

Address _____ Apt. _____

City   State/Prov.   Zip/Postal Code

Account #_____

Return entry with invoice in reply envelope.

© 1995 HARLEQUIN ENTERPRISES LTD.   CTV KAL